SHYNE BRIGHT ENTERTAINMENT

presents

KASH'D OUT

The Bluegrass Story

Part II

SHYNE BRIGHT ENTERTAINMENT

presents

KASH'D OUT

The Bluegrass Story

Part II

By Tyrene "Topp Dawg" Collins

Published by
MIDNIGHT EXPRESS BOOKS

KASH'D OUT
The Bluegrass Story
Part II

Copyright © 2013 by Tyrene "Topp Dawg" Collins

Artwork by John Puckett

ISBN-10: 0988806347
ISBN-13: 978-0-9888063-4-4

Published by
MIDNIGHT EXPRESS BOOKS
POBox 69
Berryville AR 72616
(870) 210-3772
MEBooks1@yahoo.com

KASH'D OUT
The Bluegrass Story

Part II

By Tyrene "Topp Dawg" Collins

This book is dedicated to every mother that has lost a son or daughter to this mean game that we play in. Lord knows that without ya'll, many of us wouldn't make it back here.

I am very thankful for mine!

And, a very special thanks to Midnight Express Books.

Kash'd Out

A HUSTLA'S PRAYER

Lord I come to you as humble as I can with one request. Please protect me from my friends; I'll take care of my enemies.

Amen

ACKNOWLEDGEMENTS

Hello world I'm back for a second time and having a ball while doing so. Thanks to all those who have had the time to pick my books up and read them. I had a lot of fun writing these books and for a brief moment I was free from behind these fences. I'm going to say some things here that some people really ain't going to like and some people are absolutely going to enjoy. Either way like my big partner said this is my book so I can do what I want. Now a little bit about myself so the world can have a feel about who I am. I'm serving a political debt for my whole hood and I know now that I was the only one who could do it. I smile everyday and do this one day at a time because that's the only sane way to do it and I never complain because I have seen real men who are never going home again it's a real humbling experience. I had my O.G. ask me one day what's my motivation? I told him making it home alive and going back to the top. The second part will be easy because if you're reading this book you're putting me within reach of my goal. But however this time I won't be taking the same people with me (friends, family and lovers) too much extra weight that never pays off in the end. An old white man who I meet on my journey ran something by me that I'll never forget. Pennies make dollars and dollars makes millions I didn't understand at first but I got it now so hold on to your hats and ladies please keep your dress from flying up because the sky is the limit for me.

Now I have a lot of people I want to say thanks to so please bear with me. They are very deserving of the love that I send back their way because they send it to me.

Momma - I did part II and I did it like you said. I didn't ask nobody for help because I see clearly what you were talking about. I know I could've asked you for every dollar but what you've done for me throughout my whole life is priceless. You're the best and without you Lord knows I would have never made it thus far. Thanks baby, I love you.

Carl Jr., Tammy and Robin - Anything I do ya'll always been down for my mission and that means the world to me thanks, I love ya'll.

Angie Boo and Keesha – What? Ya'll thought I forgot ya'll? Nah, never that. I love ya'll too!

Charlene - Smile for me baby! Your boy acting a plum fool again. Damn

I miss you something terrible this time around but I feel your love in my heart and that makes it okay. I love you honey, baby love; Rest In Peace.

Alaysha - Hey baby! I've watched you grow up most of your life from behind these walls and fences. What I see has put a smile on my face. Your time is coming to make your own decision please make them wisely and make us all proud. I love you always don't you ever forget it.

JahQuez - Hey buddy boy! Something that I want to share with you as day by day you're becoming a man: Loyalty and Trust is a must from anybody you allow into your life. If there is neither, you cannot have any room for them no matter who they are. Keep your head in them books and become anything your heart desires. I'll be cheerleading from the sideline rooting you to victory. I love you.

Family- I thought family was supposed to lookout for one another? I've been gone for some years now and I'm stilling waiting. I'm cool because moms 'em makes sure of that but if not me at least take care of each other. Much love from behind these walls and fences.

Now this part is going to be real good an interesting to a few so pay very close attention. This is for three women who have been a part of my life at one time or another. I won't be mentioning their names but you can bet your last dollar they know who I'm talking too.

Hey baby girl! I remember when you ask me where would we be if I never got locked up? I give you my answer but now I want to ask you something? Where would we be if you never left me when I was locked up? You be safe and take care of yourself.

Hey momma! I know I played a major role in how our situation played out and I accept that whole heartedly. Got something I really need to get off my chest because I'll feel better when I do. Was it that easy for you to leave me for dead? I don't need an answer because your actions speak for themselves. My nigga told me if you love something let it go. You be sweet. BYE baby!

Hey baby doll! First and foremost I want to say thanks. You had every right to bail when they closed that door behind me but you choose to stay and ride it out with a real nigga. I swear you're what every real nigga needs. You are Loyal, Respectful and have my best interest at heart. You are a very rare breed and I must say your Ride or Die to the fullest. I lied when I said I wasn't going to mention no names because you have earned it. Harmonie I can never repay you for what you have done but I'll do my best; I love you.

Neckbone (South Philly) - Thanks for the game you introduced me to they never seen this one coming.

To all the fellows in the library that held me down with a typewriter when I couldn't get out of the unit; thanks guys you helped me do what a lot of people said I couldn't and that's part II.

To all my God Body brothers I say one thing to you: Peace God.

All the O.G.s doing them life bids - People say they feel your pain. But that is impossible because your pain is truly unbearable. I send my love your way because you are a true general because you did not fold. May God keep your spirits high and keep standing strong.

Big Woods a.k.a Green Eyes - Like you said, "Big Bucks, no Whammies!" I got 'em watching my feet and not my hands (3-0) thanks my nigga, St. Louis should be proud of you.

To all who help put me here and those who have betrayed me while I was here TODAVIA NO ES AMOR PERDIDA, MAS DE ESO "CHINGA TU MADRE" LO QUE TU DA'S, ESPERA LO PARA TRAS! It would be in your best interest to get someone to translate that for you so you'll know: STAY THE FUCK OUT OF MY WAY upon my return!!!!

My B-Dawg niggas from all over the world - I've meet men from every corner of the U.S. and some boys that don't speak one word of English but understand that RED flag means a lot. It ain't where you're from as long as it's in your heart, that's all I'm standing on. California is the birth place but now it's worldwide. Now I'll be letting my people know I haven't forgot them.

Smooth Lane(PDL), Tiny(PDL), Tony B(PDL), The whole Pasadena Denver Lane, the LA Lanes 106, Bam(456), Way Out (Cedar Block Piru), Ike (Westside Piru) T-Roy (9-4 Family). Joe-Joe (Southside Villains), Big Los (APB), Bone (BPS), Q (Bounty Hunters), Steel Bill (Lincoln Park),

Lil Dee (62 Brims), B-Low (Swans), Moo-Moo (Denver Lane), Red (Valentine), Buck(183), Boo (Sex, Money, Murder), Smooth (Nine-Tray), Whitey (VNG), Poppa, Biggz (NHB 20's) Bazzy, Bean, Reddy, Focus, Flea, Lou, Slim-Bo, Ravi, T-Row, Snipe - look I could go on and on but I'm not. So if I left you out, I didn't mean too.

Big Chill and BT Knoxville (Tenn), ya'll know what it is all my niggas on 13th St. 300 Block Covington (KY), Teezy, Kapone, Bliss and B Tyler, we in the building. The Whole Eastside of Louisville and The Whole Eastside of Lexington Soo Woo all day!

One more person - please Amai. What? You thought I was going to leave you out? Not for nothing in the world Blood! Hold on, our turn is coming.

To every homie living and to every one of them that fell so we would be able to represent this, please stand tall. It's a cold world blood, show no mercy and ask for none in return!! Dawg or mutha-fucking die!!!

Now to my homies from all over The Bluegrass - I swear there are more then I can name, but I'm a do my best to show ya'll real niggas some love.

Tank (Lex), LilDeion (Lex), Big World (Lex), Face (Lex) Von (Lex), T.Clay (Lex), Brother B (Lex), Johnny J (Lex), Lil Brucey (Lex), B-Sting (Lex) Gease (Lex), Boogie (Lex). All the old-school gangstas that I've meet on my travels keep your head up and stay ten toes down like you told me.

Now off to The Derby City and Lord knows I can't get all you niggas names in here but I'm going to try.

Uncle Larry (Lou), Big Ben (Lou), Hub (Lou), Dirty Red (Lou), J.R. Sleazy E(Lou), Boogie(Lou), Twin (Big D Lou), Tom P. (Lou), T.Y. (Lou), J.T.(Lou), Pumpkin (Lou), Kobe (Lou), Bullet (Lou), Tyree (Lou), Fam-O (Lou &E-Ville Ind), Smooth (Lou) Griff (Lou). There are just too many, but ya'll get the picture; these my peoples and we standing with nothing but Pride.

Cash (B.G.), T-One (B.G.), Cadillac Curly(Winchester), Hawk G, The whole Paris a.k.a. 148,PKY or P-Funk ya'll niggas hold your heads - I feel your mutha fucking pain. Moody (Hop-Town), L (Hop-Town), L.A. (Hop-Town), Scrap (Hop-Town), Paducah, Owensboro, Madisonville, Franklin, Campbellville, Horse Cave, Russelville, Central City, Glasgow, E-Twon, Bardstown, Lebanon, Richmond, Danville, Frankfort, Harrodsburg, Cynthiana, Maysville, Flemingburg. The whole COMMONWEALTH OF KENTUCKY THIS IS FOR YA'LL.

Big Goo - Thanks for being my ear, letting me know that real gangstas are going to love this no matter where they're from. St. Louis stayed up for a real O.G.

Skeet - My dude, I put part two together without you. Lord knows I needed that Catholic School Education, but I managed to see it though. One love.

Da-Vee - You said do it my way and I did. But I got to steal your line on this one. This mutha fucka is colder than a broke Ho's heart! This my Detroit playa and I want to shout out Rah-Rah.

Rooster - Thanks to you for not letting me keep putting part two off. This is my Windy City partna (Chicago) Westside all day.

Silk - When I needed somebody to give me a little advice or something small you always had it. Thanks my nigga your turn is long overdue. Richmond, VA. he represents ya'll very well.

Black Al, Big H and Jordan - I got one thing to say to ya'll. Rastafarian service in progress!! (hahaha) Cincinnati, Nap-Town and Warner Robins Georgia is the home to these real niggas.

To all my soulja's who are jailed unjust, I feel your pain. To those warriors trapped in that mountain in Florence, hold tight and stand strong. USP Big Sandy, USP Terre Haute, USP Atwater, USP McCreary, USP Allenwood, USP Beaumont, USP Pollock, USP Victorville, USP Coleman 1 and 2, USP Cannan, USP Hazelton and to all the old school pens (Niggas like myself – I was a youngster then) Atlanta, the old Terre Haute, Leavenworth, Lompoc, Lewisburg and when Marion was the ADX. The walls may have our bodies trapped behind them but please keep your mind free.

Now to some place where I have comrades doing the do. This may take a second I just want to show some love: FCI Beckley, FCI Ashland, FCI Manchester, FCI Milan, FCI Elkton, FCI Otisville, FCI Fort Dix, FCI Schuykill, FCI Loretto, FCI Big Spring, FCI Seagoville, FCI Texarkana, FCI Three Rivers, FCI Bastrop, FCI Miami, FCI Estill, FCI Jesup, FCI Edgefield, FCI Yazoo City, FCI Talladega, FCI Herlong, FCI Sheridan, FCI Victorville 1 and 2, FCI Terminal Island, FCI Phoenix and Tucson. I know I left some of you out but I'm a say this because I want you in. Wherever you are housed, please hold your head up and stay strong.

There is no way I could forget about all my homies locked around The Bluegrass. North Point, EKCC, Luther Luckett, KSR, Lee Co. Green River, RCC, Little Sandy, KSP Eddyville, Marion Co. Blackburn, Frankfort, Pee-Wee Valley and Western. What ladies? You thought I forgot about the most precious jewel on earth I seriously doubt it. I've been where you've been I felt your pain and struggles. All you can do is do it one day at a time.

Solo (Nutty Black), Smoke (Rollin 60's), Fresh (Eight-Tray), Slow (Hoover), Ice (Venice Sho Line), Johnny Boy (Grape Street), Chicken (Avlon), Kadafi (Harlem Rollin 30's). Walk for me after this.

GEORGETOWN KENTUCKY - My home-base, what you thought I forgot about ya'll? Ain't no way in the world I could let ya'll get away without saying what on my mind. So please hold on for a few more moments so I can get this off my chest. To all the homies who have been to the FEDS, or still in like myself, I say to you that you represented very well on your travel because I know people who have spoke very highly of you. Thanks to the few people who have sent a little love my way or just asked my peoples about me.

Now I'll be giving a little history lesson to you since I know most of you didn't pay attention in history class but I had a little help on this one myself. Thanks to a good friend of mine (Chief Two Moons from Sioux Falls South Dakota, by way of Eagle Butte Cheyenne River Sioux Tribe). When the Native American's were fighting to keep their land the best warriors they had were called Dog Soldiers. See I am the very best Dog Soldier that Georgetown Kentucky has to offer we a few but I am the best. Yard to yard, city to city I put my hood on my back without a hint of hesitation or regret. That's why I get the love and respect that I do, 'cause I earned it. This is one guarantee that the world most know. I PUT ON FOR MY CITY! My crown has dust on it and my throne is empty but rest to sure I bow out gracefully. From where I sit and watch the game I don't see none of you trying to win. If you're not in it to win it please do yourself and the people who love you a favor get on the bench with me voluntarily because if these people (FEDS) put you there I know it ain't ONE of you who can stand it. Sometime certain shoes are not made to be filled its still ONE LOVE from the boss.

Mr. Fletcher - All the thanks in the world goes to you because you keep this ragged ass type- writer they give us to use rolling so I could do what people said I couldn't do. Thanks old man, you're a true outlaw.

To all my beautiful ladies all around the Federal BOP I didn't forget about ya'll only a fool would do that. Most of you rode out with your dude and some of you took the fall for him either way I'll let you know one thing. You're the cream of the crop nothing even comes close. FCI Dublin, FMC Carswell, FCI Danbury ,FPC Alderson, FPC Atwood, and especially all of you at the FCI in Tallahassee, Florida. Stand strong and hold your head high there is bunch of real niggas who wished they had you. Brandi and Melizza, smile for a real nigga.

Rock – Houston, Texas. When you say money ain't a thang, you meant it. Thanks for supporting my hustle all the way around.

Last but really should've been first all real men no matter what color you are. They winning (suckas) and it's 4th and long. I'll say this then I'm gone Suckas get lucky; Hustlas don't stand a chance. GOD BLESS YOU ALL AND HOLD TIGHT OUR TURN WILL COME....

STOLEN DREAMS

What I'm about to say is USDA certified by real Hustlas, Gangstas and Head Bustas. They told me to make sure I let the world know how real men feel. So I'm about to give you suckas out there some knowledge from every soldier that is behind these walls and fences. There is a couple things that should've happened to you and I'm about to let you know. First and foremost your Daddy should've gotten some head and your Momma should've swallowed you but since that bitch was being lazy do the world a favor and kill yourself. See if you took offense to this your one of those sucka-ass niggas I'm talking about out there in the way of a real niggas hopes and dreams…

Soo Woo

CHAPTER 1

I've never been on a plane before but the FEDS help fix that problem ASAP. Hell they put us all on planes and transport us all over the country. My first stop was Oklahoma City; I got in a bit of trouble out there fucking with my cell-mate. He was a little wild ass young nigga from Baton Rouge Louisiana that everybody called Gator.

"Gator my nigga, why don't you chill for second with this flooding the tier shit!"

"Man fuck that! These crackers just give me1200 months! I can't do all that mutha fucking time!"

Let me tell you a little bit about Gator. He killed an off-duty police officer in a bank robbery gone bad. His old man got the death penalty. So I guess I'll just lay back and see what's going to happen.

It didn't take long. Shit is about to get real interesting because these hillbillies just showed up with a video camera!

"Mr. Shyne, please come to the food port and cuff up now!"

Now I know these crackers are out their rabbit-ass minds! To think I'm going to cuff up with this young nigga going bananas up in this bitch. So I do what any real nigga would do.

"Man fuck ya'll come on in here and get us!"

Well we didn't have to wait long because the cell extraction team was all ready to go. Believe me "go" is exactly what they did. Seven of the biggest crackers in the world hit that door. I could lie and tell you me and Gator won but I won't. They fucked us around up in that cell. By the time they were done, I had a dislocated shoulder and four broken ribs.

I didn't see Gator after that but I heard he got sent to the ADX. That's the super-max in Florence, Colorado. Me, I landed at the USP in Terre

Haute, Indiana and I got put in cell block E, right next to the Death Row. My cell mate was this young nigga from Columbia, South Carolina; we called him Kev-O.

"Look, don't unroll that bed roll until I take you to your home boys!"

"What you mean by that?"

"You ain't my homie, so I don't know what they might want to do about you."

I would learn later that I had two weeks to get my paperwork sent in so they could determine whether or not I could stay on the yard.

"I'm 'a give you a few things until after count, then I'm going to take you to your peoples, but I want my shit back!"

He gave me some goodies and an old pair of shoes and a towel rolled up. That threw me for a loop until I opened it. The home-made knife that was in it would go in the front and be hanging out the back.

We kicked it until after count was over, then he took me to a group of guys that were standing around kicking it, so we waited until we were acknowledged.

"Hey fellas this my celly but he's ya'lls home boy so I brought him to ya'll."

"What's up young'un? I'm Moon; what's your name and were you from?"

"Name's Dawg and I'm from Georgetown."

Moon was an older guy and he was from Louisville. He looked at Kev-O and then back to me.

"Kev you tell him the rules?"

"Yeah I ran it down to him but he only got two weeks with me."

"Well two weeks it is. Now what do we owe you?"

"Nothing O.G. - just want my hammer back."

16

"We'll give him one so get yours back. Thanks for bringing him to us."

Kev-0 doesn't say much after that he just eased off. I stayed with all my homies from Kentucky. There wasn't many, only about 17 in all from all over The Bluegrass. After I got back to my cell for lock down me and Kev-O kicked it some more.

"Dawg this your first day so I warn you keep your mouth shut and your eyes open! This a mutha fucking war zone! Bloods, Crips, G.D.'s, Vice Lords, A. B's and let's not forget the Mexicans."

"I'm'a be straight."

"Don't let shit fool you understand! Shit is boiling over right now as we speak."

"Alright I'm a keep my eyes open."

"You better for your own health."

The lights went out and I laid on my bunk thinking about all kinds of shit. But I caught myself praying to God for the first time in my life; I didn't ask for much just a little guidance.

March 1999

I took care of that paperwork thing and was allowed to stay on the yard. I've been up here for a few months and shit is as wild as Kev said it was. Some of my homies have been shipped to other prison Moon got sent down to the F.C.I. in Manchester Kentucky Slim got sent to the F.C.I. in Ashland Kentucky. So I've been hanging with the homies who are left and this real O.G. nigga from Washington D.C. his name is Head-Bey. We're playing chess in his cell and I'm talking shit.

"Head-Bey why you always mumbling to yourself when you're about to make a move?"

He doesn't say anything at first so I wait because I know if I say something else he'll say I talk too much. When he does finally make his move I knew the game was over.

"Checkmate big mouth! Now get on up and throw that combo that

Kurtz-El showed you a 100 times without taking a break."

"Come on Head-Bey! I did that combo for three straight hours yesterday my shoulders hurt!"

"See that's your problem! If I can get your heart as big as your mouth you would be dangerous! Now get your country ass up and get busy!"

Damn I stand up and walked to the cell door. Got to see where the C.O. is at. I don't see him so I squared up and started my combo: 1, 2, 4. For those who don't know, that's a jab, jab, right hook. Head-Bey sat back and watched me like he's the best trainer in the world. Halfway threw I started to feel real light on my feet so I start putting my foot work into play and bobbing my head. By the time I turned all the way back around Head-Bey was smiling and let me tell you smiling is something he rarely does.

"So what do you think about that Head-Bey?"

"Boy you looked good but you better ask him what he thinks."

Without thinking I spun on my heels right back into my fighting stance. I already knew who was behind me and boy was I right. He shot a straight jab out so fast it almost caught me flat footed I side step it and shot one back. We tested each other until Head-Bey had seen enough.

"Time!"

"Kurtz-El why you always starting shit every time I see you?"

"Keep you ready for battle Slim and day by day I see you're almost there."

That made me feel good coming from Kurtz-El. Hell he's a two time golden gloves champ out of Congress Park that in Southeast Washington D.C. he just couldn't keep that pistol out his hand got 40 years under the old law.

"Thanks Kurtz-El but I'm 'bout to go watch the NCAA National Championship game. You know my girl Cee-Cee is playing tonight!"

"Boy you've been chasing that girl all over TV all year! She got your nose wide open!"

"Nah it ain't like that she's my people and we go back that's all"

By now Head-Bey and Kurtz-El were talking so I bailed out. On my way to watch the game I pass Kev-O.

"What's up Dawg were you going?"

"To watch the game why what's up?"

"Let's go smoke some of this kill I got!"

"Nigga you know that's right up my alley!"

We put the smoke up in the air and shit was good. So I make my way to the TV and their doing the starting line ups and that shit put a smile on my face to see Cee-Cee run out on that court. By the time the game was over Cee-Cee and her team had won. 62-45 I had a great feeling watching my child hood friend play on the big stage I went to bed that night on a high note!

> The true meaning of
> Dear John and on top
> of real bad news...........

The summer rolled around and I've not heard from Faye or Randi. Can't much blame 'em for not fucking with me but damn I was a pretty good dude on the streets. I've not seen Head-Bey today he had a call out to medical. On my way to do pull ups I see him but he's walking with his hoimes from D.C. so I stayed back. I'll get with him later. I went to mail call today don't know why I don't get much mail but I went anyways. Well, I'll damn, what do you know I got a letter from Faye. As I make my way back to my cell I got to pass Head-Bey cell and him and Kurtz-El were in there talking, so I stop and wait for him to tell me to come in.

"Come on in Slim been waiting on you to get back from mail call."

"What's up ya'll?"

"You get any mail today?"

"Yeah my girl finally got at me but I ain't read it yet."

"Well son got some news today that wasn't too good."

I don't say shit cause I've learn to keep my mouth shut when Head-Bey was talking cause that when all the game and knowledge would be coming out.

"They told me I have cancer. They want to send me down to the Medical Center in Butner, North Carolina."

"Damn Bey can they fix it?"

He doesn't say nothing and Kurtz-El got a far off look on his face.

"Don't know son guess I'll leave it in Allah's hands."

"I'm sorry to hear that what can I do?"

"Nothing but you better defend yourself."

Wasn't no need to ask what he was talking about so I got in my stance. Kurtz-El popped to his feet so fast that when I blinked he was within range for me to shoot a short jab. I paid a great price for leaving it hanging out there too long. Now sense we've been shadow boxing he has never hit me but .I learned something valuable today. That fool hit me with a body shot that sent me to the cell floor. Shit knocked the wind out of me. Kurtz-El helped me up and Head-Bey give me a lesson in life I would never forget.

"You got to be prepared for the unthinkable in life. Got to figure out your next move before you need it, understand!"

I sat there letting what he said sink in.

"I'll be leaving Thursday and we might as well tell you Kurtz-El is going to the F.C.I. in Cumberland Maryland So you got to stay sharp physically and mentally. No time for that playing around cause your life is on the line!"

"I'll be okay Head-Bey you just keep your faith."

"You know what young'un? I knew this day would come but it's hard to believe 1969 I walked into prison and now my biggest fear well hell my only fear may be my reality."

"What you talking about Head-Bey?"

"Dying old and lonely in one of these hell holes!" Nobody said nothing so we all sat around in our own thoughts. Finally Head-Bey said, "Show me a 1, 2, 1, 4 and I want it sharp and clean so don't stop until I say so."

I did that not playing much attention to the time until I heard the C.O. call lockdown.

"I'll see ya'll tomorrow after breakfast."

"Okay Slim you be easy and guard your heart."

Head-Bey always says the damnest things. Back to my cell Kev-O was sitting on his bunk listening to his radio. I hop up on my bunk with my letter in my hand. I smelled the letter first; no scent. I look at it, front and back. I guess it's time to open it up and see what's inside.

> Dear, Telly.
>
> Hello. Hope your okay. I'm fine just going to class and trying to live life. I'm not going to be long so please understand were I'm coming from on this. I have a lot of living to do so I won't be seeing or writing you no more. I hope you understand you'll always have a spot in my heart. You take care of yourself in there.
>
> Love, Faye

Damn talking about blunt and straight to the point. I knew this day would come she goes to Kentucky State. Niggas going to be at her just like every other female on that campus. Man, fuck it! I got to stay focus on doing this time Like Head-Bey said time heals everything. So by the time I hit the streets she'll be a distant member. NO LOVE LOST!!!

Time waits for no one!!

Head-Bey and Kurtz-El have been gone for about eight months now. So

I stay sharp like Head-Bey said. Two hours a day I shadow box an all Kev-O does is shake his big old head. They put me in for a transfer but my destination hasn't came back yet. Fresh off the pull up bar minding my own business this young nigga Money from Des Moines Iowa started popping slick. I try to pay it no never mind but niggas take shit way to far.

"Man these backwoods ass niggas be in the way!"

He's with a couple of his homies so the odds are stacked against me but fuck it I'm trained to go!!!

"Nigga put a name on that statement you wheat growing ass nigga!"

I see him look at his homies like the bitch he really is. See the word is he had some real paper on the streets..

"I'm a dust that ass off country nigga!"

"You got that to do mutha fucka!"

He started making his way towards me with his homies in tow. But for some strange reason all them fools stopped dead in their tracks. I took a quick look over my shoulder and I see the Blood niggas from California standing no less than two or three yards away from me. I've talked to the big nigga standing up front his name is Big Tone. He says the damndest thing you ever wanted to hear.

"Lil Blood going to get a fair one while ain't none of his homeboyz around or we all going to the mutha fucking bucket today!"

Now I knew without a doubt I had to put some major knots on this fool's head. I got half the Blood car backing me and I don't know why? I hope all that shit Head-Bey and Kurtz –El taught me pays off.

" Bring yo ass big mouth! It's just you and me fag mutha fucka!"

This nigga looked like he might know how to get down but looks are very deceiving. Just like I did he hung his jab out there way too long and I tapped that chin twice. I backed up to let him get his self together I'm going to embarrass this nigga in front of his homies. He came at me like a wild man. It shouldn't have been that easy. I've learn to remain calm and shit seemed to be moving in slow motion. Hell nobody I mean nobody is as fast as Kurtz-El so dude had nothing coming but a good old fashion country ass whopping! I side stepped him and shot a over hand right to his ear and down he went. I started making my way toward him so I could put my boots on his head but Big Tone stopped me.

"Are you ready to kill him?"

"Nah just going to step on his mutha fucking head a little bit!"

"Any time you stomp a man be prepared to kill him understand me!?"

"Yeah whatevea thanks for getting me a fair one."

"Nah Damu, all the thanks goes to you."

They watched me as I walked back towards my cell-block. Hell a few of them lived in there anyways but what he said wouldn't dawn on me until me and Kev-O talked later that night. Damn the homies from Kentucky going to be mad-ass a mutha fucka!!!!

Getting scolded
and learning the truth

After count I went to the gym so I could catch up with my homies from The Bluegrass. Bear and J. Black make all the calls since Moon left and both them fools are from Lexington. So I knew I would get an ear full with me being from Georgetown that's only 14 miles away. We started kicking it I knew J. Black wouldn't say much hell he never says much to think of it. He's always scheming on how to rob another bank when he gets home Bear is the one going to chew my ass out.

"Dawg what were you thinking? Fighting without none of us around?"

"Didn't have time to wait shit bubbled over too fast and I had to get busy right then and there!"

"Do you know you just got right in the middle of a fucking gang war country ass nigga!"

"How the fuck was I suppose too know Bear!"

"If you pay more attention to what's going on around you like you do your fucking boxing you would know!"

"So what we going to do about it?"

"Whatevea them pussy ass niggas want to do! Damn I'll be glad when they ship your young wild ass!"

By this time the gym was feeling up I see the Bloods and their signaling for me to come over. I look at J. Black and he shakes his head yeah so I make my way over to them. All eyes were on me as I did so. Big Tone was there but he ain't their shot caller. A nigga named Top-Dolla is and he's with them. When I got over there I didn't say shit so he spoke first.

"Damn lil homie, my homeboyz tell me you got a big heart about to try all them marks by yourself!"

"It wasn't nothing special just me standing up for myself."

"Well you did us a favor so we going to do you one. I know them niggas are mad look at them."

I followed his finger to where that punk and a lot more of his homies were sitting and they looked mad as hell.

"Go tell Bear we got you until you leave."

"Why?"

"It's for your own health and theirs too!"

I look at the number of my homies from Kentucky and it was short I mean real short. I know all these niggas would go but why put them in harm's way for the shit I done without nobody's okay. I got love for them so I made my decision right then and there.

"Okay Dolla let me go holla at them."

I made my way back over to the home team I talk to all of them about what's going down and everybody gives me their blessing. So Bear stood up and stuck his hand out I shook it then he pulled me close so I was the only one who could hear what he had to say.

"With them backing you in here or on the streets you'll see and do things you've never dreamed of."

It would take me five more years to understand what Bear was talking about and boy would he be right. I go back to where all the Bloods were sitting and they sat me next to Dolla. We watched the game until yard re-call. I walked back to the cell-block with Pusha, Tiny and Tony Redd. Once in my cell Kev-O was just shaking that big old head of his.

"What you doing that for?"

"Man do you know what the fuck you just done?"

"Fuck it I'll be leaving soon anyways."

"Nigga what happens if they turn your transfer down and you got to stay!"

"I'll get in where I fit in fool!"

"Man that nigga you jumped on ain't really from Iowa he's from Cali. Done some real bad shit out west and the Bloods and Crips want him dead but the G.D's are backing him cause he got major paper and plus he's tied to a Untied States Congressman somehow."

"Well why don't they just kill him then?"

"It's ain't that easy. Prison politics won't allow it right now so everybody got to wait until another time."

"Man this shit is crazy! Hope my transfer hurries up and comes on though."

"Man who you telling! I need your wild ass to get in the wind!"

Me and Kev-O talked and smoked some of that good green he's been having here lately. He thinks I don't pay attention to nothing but my boxing but I know he's fucking that pretty little case manager. When I did close my eyes that night, all I could see was money piling to the moon. That dream wouldn't be my reality for a few more years. Three weeks later an a whole bunch of prison tattoo's later I was back in Oklahoma City waiting on a plane ride to the F.C.I. in Beckley West

Virginia.

CHAPTER 2

February 2000
a very short stay
in the coal mountains of West VA...

My stay in Oklahoma City was a lot longer than the first time But what could I do but lay my ass down. I finally make it to Beckley and there was triple the amount Kentucky niggas down there. Some nigga name Wal-Doe had the keys to the car. I lived in Pine-B lower with the homie Puke-Rat. Shit was okay until this one loud mouth nigga from Cleveland Ohio came down from the USP in Lewisburg Pennsylvania. I would see him disrespecting all over the compound a lot. This fool must got a death wish with all these D.C. niggas running around this bitch. I do my regular pull ups and run the track, But today I'm going to call home got to see what Charlene is up too. The phone rang a couple of times then she finally picked up After all the formality my phone line goes live.

"What's up Charlene?"

"You little bitch what took you so long to call me?"

"Them crackers had me out west sitting until the weather broke."

"Well they say Keith and Ray are on their way up there were you're at any day."

"Oh yeah that would be straight. I ain't seen nobody from home in awhile."

Charlene was rumbling on about this and that but I wanted to know a few things.

"Charlene were they sending Nation Wide, too?"

"Up to Morgantown and Freddie's in Lexington with their old asses They know better!"

"Digg that but check this out you seen Randi bailing through there?"

"Look ugly ass boy! Don't be worrying about no broad while you're doing time. It could cost you your life. Plus they going to do what they want anyways you understand me!?"

"Yeah baby I hear you. What it look like around there?"

"Niggas broke and scared to make a dollar. I hear there some Cincinnati niggas over in The Heights getting a little paper."

Now that caught me by surprise. They let some out of towners get some money that's hard to believe. Well I'll have to take a look at them fools if they're still around when I touchdown.

"Them niggas soft over there anyways! They better not bring they ass over on our side."

"I thank they know better. Snoop told me to ask you did you get your pictures?"

"Yeah I gott'em. Tell'em I said send some more. Well love, bout to go. I'll call in a couple of weeks."

"Okay baby, don't take so long next time, you little ugly thang!"

"I won't. I love you!"

"Love you honey, baby, love!"

I always feel good after talking to Charlene.

Now time to go to the gym. I want to see this nigga they call Sports Center play Want to see if he's as good as they say. I heard tells of another nigga name Silk up at Allenwood's USP said he might be better than MJ. Hard to believe but niggas been talking about him for years. By the time the game was over the boy Sport Center went bananas in that gym Can't lie the boy got game.

Springtime, 2000
On the move once again!!

They getting ready for the summer time softball league and the homie Wal-Doe a mutha fucka. Kentucky, Tennessee and OH-dime (OHIO) got a team together It was late night and me and Smiley were locked in the TV room, plus that big mouth nigga from Cleveland. Yeah that's right what you niggas call bubble or bus stops use to be TV rooms. That nigga was bumping his gum together something terrible So Smiley with that same kool-aid smile on his face leaned over and whispered.

"Dawg you got your knife?"

I couldn't lie to him this my partner Hell truth be told I got two knifes on me. My nigga Bub he's from Fayetteville North Carolina he give me his before he went to the camp yesterday. Damn Smiley doing a 15 to 45 year sentence for murder one.

"Yeah my nigga I got it."

"Well the fuck is you waiting on!?"

DAMN. I just got here but like Head-Bey said be prepared for the unthinkable at all times. I'm not going to say what happen in that TV room. All I know is that big mouth had so many holes in him only the Lord could save that fool. And I be damned if that fool didn't make it. Off to the SHU (special housing unit) SIS was on my ass from the jump talking about sending it outside court. Fuck it I'm a play it how it goes.

13 months later and
we're still on lockdown!!!!

Would you believe it, they still got us in the SHU. The United States District Attorney in Beaver West Virginia said he got better stuff to do beside prosecute a couple of niggers trying to kill each other Hell let him tell it we were doing the whole world a favor. So the real word is big mouth wouldn't testify Bitch ass nigga got sent to the Medical spot in Lexington Kentucky. Damn I know now I won't be going that way They got a better trip in store for me. Rec time so I know Big Blue is coming out and he wants to hear the same old shit about the TV room. Blue's from Long Beach California He's on a disciplinary way out here and by the looks of thing he's about to be on another one. He don't give a fuck he's doing a life sentence.

"Dawg what's up young nigga?"

"Ain't nothing O.G. wishing they hurry the fuck up with these transfers!"

"Don't trip lil homie, the destinations fell though early this morning We all about to roll!"

He thinks he's slick hollering that roll shit. He's a Rollin 20 Crip I'll catch him on the rebound. I hope they send me down to the F.C.I in Manchester Kentucky but I know my luck ain't that good. Later that day I found out I was going to the F.C.I in Sheridan Oregon Can you believe that shit!

Two weeks later we left West Virginia Down to Atlanta to the hold over I meet an old school jack boy from Cashville Tenn. A Key (Nashville Tennessee) name Slaw. He was always talking that gangsta shit and young niggas like myself loved every second of it. Today was a little different than the other days.

"Yeah young nigga if you want a nigga to tell you where's the money and the work at when you run up in his spot fuck shooting him. Don't even slip him upside his head with the pistol. Duck tape that nigga up and stick a hot curling iron up his ass! That fool going to tell you whatevea you need to know."

Everybody laughed even myself but on some real shit I was putting that one in my member bank for later uses. I make it to Oklahoma City and a week later I was in Oregon. I hit the compound knowing I wouldn't have a homeboy in sight But to my unknowing mind I would have plenty real soon. On my way from R&D to my assigned unit A-3. Now I've been around niggas from all over the world but these niggas are different West Coast all day. My celly is from Pasadena California and we hit it right off His name is Shakey.

"What's up homie? Where are you from?"

"A small town in Kentucky."

"Oh shit! You're the young nigga that was at Terre Haute with Pusha'em."

Now that had my ears up. How would this nigga know that? The look on my face must have given away what I was thinking.

"Man Pusha got here a few months back telling us what was going on down there. I'll bet my life you're the nigga he was talking about!"

"Where's he at? I need to see him ASAP!"

"Well get up with them niggas after count."

After count we went to the rec yard and the group of niggas we pulled up on was well over a 100 Shakey was about to say something when Pusha looked up and saw me.

"Man what the fuck my nigga! How you get way out here?"

"Got in some real deep shit in West Virginia so here I am."

We shook up an all the other homies were looking at us like we were nuts. So Pusha told them how I got down for my flag I thought I was about to have to get busy again with some of these niggas.

"Look ya'll I understand if ya'll ain't got no room for me."

When I said that, this real old looking nigga with two long as braids in his hair stepped to the front.

"Take your shirt off Blood."

I looked at that nigga like he was crazy. A couple of those niggas started circling me. I couldn't win but I would do my best to break at least one these niggas' jaw.

"I want to see if you're the one my baby brother was talking about."

"Who's your brother?"

"Big Tone fool!"

Damn that's the big homie who showed me that love that day up at Terre Haute. So I took my shirt off. The tattoo's on my stomach, back and arms told a story all by themselves to those who knew what they were looking that.

"Nah Damu, we got plenty room for you."

"Thanks O.G. what's your name?"

"T. Banks."

"I'm Dawg."

"I know who you are. Got a picture of ya'll from The Haute. Tone was crazy about your young country ass."

"Where they got him at now?"

"He's at the USP in Lompoc."

"I need me a hammer and some shoes until my property lands."

With one look at this young nigga, he had to be younger than me, he gives me a knife. Later, me and him would become the best of friends His name is On-One a name that a really earned.

November 2002 Heading
back to The Bluegrass...

Man these last 16 months has flown by Got mad love for these Cali niggas cause they've loved me back. T. Banks went home about 8 months ago and he looked out for everybody. One night before he left he had me come to his cell This talk would change my life forever.

"Dawg this is very important what I'm about to say to you. So keep it to yourself understand."

"I hear you Banks."

"Tone asked me to put you on if you wanted to get some money and leave that bank robbery shit alone. He said he didn't want you to end up like him."

Let me tell you about Big Tone. He ain't never coming home again got life for a bank robbery gone bad. That's why he took a liking to me I'll put the 211 game into full swing at the drop of a hat.

"Got to be honest with you Banks I ain't got no money to get on with when I touchdown."

"Country nigga who said you had to have some money!"

"What you're going to send me some work all the way to Kentucky!?"

"Listen and listen good! I got work in 10 states, fool! I've been getting paper since the 70's. I'm here for tax evasion, so please believe I can send it wherever it got to go!"

I let that shit soak in for a second. By the looks of this nigga, I would have never guessed that's what he was locked up for. See that's what I get for judging a book by its cover I would get the same treatment later on down the road.

"I'm going to wait on my main man Bugz to get home so I'll have some help."

"I don't care what you do Know one thing my nigga. If I send something down there it got blood on it. Not one dollar short or I'll send a bunch of spaced out cowboys down there to clean up."

Did this nigga just treating me? He got life fucked up! I ain't got on problem feeding them niggas to the hoggs. Now my turn to set the record straight.

"Banks I'm grateful for the offer I'll keep it in mind but I ain't no play thang myself. So if I did take you up on it I wouldn't play with your money cause I don't like it when somebody plays with mine! Plus me and my man would kill every nigga you send down our way."

"Now I see why Tone liked your country ass. Here is a number it hasn't changed in twenty years but only use it if you want to get paid."

"I understand."

"Much love Damu!"

"Without a doubt Blood."

So now I sit in the hole cause Kentucky Department of Corrections got a holder on me. The Scott County Sheriffs are going to make that long ass drive way up here any day. I was deep in thought when it was broke. This old pimp nigga from Milwaukee Wisconsin his name is Pretty Pie and he was kicking his pimping. Hell he was always doing that shit but today it different.

"Dawg you paying attention to this! Young nigga I use to charge mutha fuckas for this pimping!"

"What you talking about now Pie!"

"See it's about to be your turn rather you go home today or after you go to the state Either way you got to be ready!"

"Man I've been ready since day one!"

"Nah young pimping you haven't so pay attention."

"What the fuck you mean by that!"

"I've been watching you for a minute and you got what it takes to make people love you. I see the way those young niggas follow you around."

It never dawned on me how close some of them have been hanging by myside.

"See some people have it and most don't but you got it young pimping!"

"Got what Pie? Get to your point old nigga!"

"See that's the problem with you young niggas! Always in a mutha fucking rush! But I'll tell you what you got young nigga! Charisma, Razzle Dazzle and Pizzazz all wrapped up in one. Ho's going to love you and niggas going to follow your lead but there will be those back biting, hating ass niggas who'll pray for your down fall. The machine that your apart of is well oiled T. Banks is a stone cold killer. Don't let that tax evasion charge fool you young nigga!"

"Man is you preaching to me?"

"Hold up young nigga I ain't done yet! I've watched you put in work since you've got here but it's a far from over. You'll have to put in some major work on the streets so don't hesitate for one second cause it may cost you your life. It's a different ball game in California then in Kentucky so act accordingly when the time present its self understand me!"

All that was major pimping to its finest Pie really put something on my mind. Just another lesson I'll put in my member bank for later use.

"Pie when I get my bank right I'm a reach for you my nigga."

"Nah pimping don't worry about me. I got 20 months left an I'm going to get me a stable full of bad young white bitches and work'em from Frisco to Maine you understand me!"

"Pimping ain't dead them ho's just being miss lead!"

"That's right young pimping we don't chase ho's we replace them. When she breaks bad she did you a favor because she gives a qualified bitch the opportunity to get some real pimping in her life. Always remember your paper comes first and keep your dick out of them if they ain't with your program. Plus keep your pistol in a bitch niggas face and never, I mean never, come up short on your paper chase you got at!"

"You can bet yo last dollar I won't be losing this time around."

"If Las Vegas was taking that bet I would bet the ranch on you young nigga cause I know something that the whole world don't!"

"Well they bout to find out real mutha fucking soon!"

Chapter 3

March 2003
14 more months
just a minor setback
for the Dawg!!!

Can you believe these crazy ass hillbillies! They drove all the way to Oregon just to get me. Man we drove straight back to Kentucky they took turns so they could hurry up and get my black ass back in front of the judge. Back in the Scott County Detention Center I wouldn't go to court until the first Monday of the month. The courtroom was packed to capacity just to see the Dawg. I would be the last nigga to go before the judge and by the time I got up there that punk mutha fucka was mad as hell. So it took all of thirty seconds to tell me I got to see the parole board. Straight to La Grange to the fish tank. Once there it's back to normal operation for me and that's doing time. I seen the board and this fag ass nigga Steve Winburn give me a 14 month set back. I took mines and kept it pimping I knew one thing for sure I was going home the next time I saw these mutha fuckas. Once back to my housing unit all the niggas I've became cool with was waiting on me to tell them what happen. I said nothing at first but then my nigga Big World came back from commissary He's from the East Side of Lexington.

"Big homie they give me something lite."

"Ain't nothing you can't handle my nigga Give you a little more time to get ready."

"Fuck that! I'm ready now!"

"Don't bark at me Blood! You should've barked at that fag ass nigga Winburn!"

"My fault blood I'm tired of niggas saying I need more time to get ready Hell I'm ready now!"

"I know blood just hold on your turn is coming up."

Damn he's right can't be mad at him Just got to wait my turn. Shit is a straight animal house down here All these young niggas from Louisville, Lexington, Covington, Hop-Town, Bowling Green hell from all over the state. They got star wars dates and it don't even seem to be fazing them. I knew I was going back to

Eddyville but luck was on my side for the first time in a long time. Eastern Kentucky Correctional Complex, a.k.a. The Pink Palace. Don't let the name fool you Once there they housed me in dorm 8 with this old nigga from Lexington name Keg-Head.

"Dawg we going to Blackburn real soon, you watch and see what I'm telling you!"

Blackburn is a state prison in Lexington my luck can't be that good. I heard my nigga violated his parole said he was on his way up there. Bugz has been home for 2 years now heard shit tight out there for him. I know what he's waiting on and that's me. We're going to set the city on fire ASAP.

"Keg, you're just talking! Did you take your medicine this morning? We ain't going down there."

"Yeah, I took my medicine! See that's the problem with you young niggas ya'll don't pay attention to shit but that damn B.E.T.! If you watch something else on that TV you would know what's going on!"

"I know one thang, we ain't going to Blackburn Keg."

"Young fool, they're trying to turn this place into the new state penitentiary!"

"I'll believe it when I see it. Until then, stall me out with that bullshit."

"They're going to make your country-ass a believer real mutha fucking soon!"

July 9, 2003
Blackburn next stop home!!

Well I'll be damn! Old Keg-Head knew what he was talking about. They sent us to Blackburn Correctional Complex. I was so close to home, I could smell momma's cooking.

Fresh off the bus, I get put in C-2. That's the unit next to the interstate. I can look out the window and see the interstate sign that reads I-75 North to Georgetown or Cincinnati.

The first thing I do is call Charlene. After a couple of rings, she picks up.

"Beamer, what's up baby!?"

"Quit all that yelling boy! I know your little ugly ass is at Blackburn!"

Damn how would she know? I haven't called anybody yet.

"How you know that, Beamer?"

"I know everything boy! Plus these young, fast-ass girls be all in your business."

"Who's all in my business like that?"

"Look boy you can get on the computer a website called grapevine and find out where you're housed and when you go up for parole. Now does that answer your question?"

"Nah it don't! Now who told you that?"

"Hold up little boy! Watch who you're talking too like that! I ain't none of your little girlfriends, understand me?"

"Yeah I understand I'm sorry baby."

"Now that's more like it! Now let me see since you thought you were all that before you left I guess I've heard it four different times already this morning before you even called."

I wonder who it is? Fuck it. I'll find out soon enough. I know the parole board is going to let me go this time around and shit going to be on.

"Yeah they said that little black bitch Bugz is on his way up there!"

"I hope so. I ain't seen my nigga in years."

"Look here boy don't you two little bitches be up there on that bullshit getting into trouble you hear me!"

"We ain't! I see the board in April."

"Didn't I just tell you I know everything boy! I know when you go up. Is Michael up there?"

"Yeah I seen him when I got off the bus said he would get with me later."

"Well love, I'm about to cook for these nosey-ass broads who have been all in my conversation since you've called."

"Who's over there anyway?"

"Crystal, Shan and your girl Randi!"

I got quiet for a brief moment.

"Hello, hello Dawg you still there, love?"

"Yeah baby, I'm here but peep this, I got to go. You be sweet. I love you!"

"You don't want to holla at none of them?"

"Nah I'm cool tell them I said what's up?"

"Alright honey baby, love. Remember what I said and you and Bugz be good."

"I got you, be sweet."

I hung up but I could still hear her saying something but my mind was elsewhere. Damn I ain't heard from Randi in years. I know life goes on but I wasn't dead just locked in the FEDS.

August 16 2003
Long time no see

Got up early this morning; today is mom's birthday so I got to call her.

On my way to the gym to workout with my nigga Black (he's from Paris a.k.a. 148, PKY or P-Funk, however you want to call it) and Snoody, he's from The Derby City (Louisville) and half the city wants to kill this young nigga.

The bus was supposed to be here today. Wonder if my nigga is going to be on it. After working out, I holla at my old homie from The Town.

"Damn Michael. you getting fat-ass a mutha fucka!"

"Don't you worry about me young'un you just keep doing what you're doing cause you know all these young wild niggas look up to you cause you just came from the FEDS."

"What's that got to do with anything?"

"That and that big ass tattoo you got across your stomach."

I look down at my tat BLOOD big ass day across it. I always take my shirt off to flex after working out. Hell, I got that move from my old school partner Mr. Johnny he's from Louisville. See all these young niggas gang bang so I do what I've always done Fly my flag and REPRESENT!!!

"Nah, you tripping bout that one!"

"Now you listen and listen good! Those niggas from Victory Park (that's in Louisville an all them niggas is Crips) they want to get Lil Snoody but they know you, Teezy and Kapone (them my niggas from Covington 300 Block 13st) plus all the rest of them niggas who follow behind you will go war if you say so. All I ask is you to watch what you're doing because your too close to seeing the board to have a gang riot charge on your file."

"I hear you homie."

"Nah your young ass need to be listening!"

Later that day......

After lunch me, Black and Teezy were on our way to the basketball courts when the mutha fucking grey goose (the prison bus) came bailing straight though the compound. We stopped and watched as it went by and can you believe this. That black ass nigga was looking right at me. A small smile creped across his face and mine too.

"Black, there goes my nigga!"

"Look man, get that nigga straight about me and you!"

See Georgetown and Paris got a beef from way back. I don't know what it's over but 9 out 10 times, it's on sight when we see each other. But not now this nigga is good peoples, plus his brother Two was up Beckley with me.

"I got you my nigga shit's cool."

"I'm letting you know now if he starts that bullshit we're getting the fuck away from here ASAP!"

"Yeah, yeah let's go to the clothing house so I can get up with him."

"Nah, I'll get at you later."

"Teezy what's up you going or what?"

"Nah Damu, I'm going to hoop."

"Digg, I'll get up with ya'll later."

"Alright Baby Juice, later."

That nigga Black calls me everything. It's a new name every day I would catch myself using them later down the road. But for now, time to catch up with my nigga Bugz. I waited outside the clothing house for about 30 minutes before he walked out.

"Bout time black boy!"

"You know how it's goes my nigga."

We hugged and started walking back up the hill.

"What unit they put you in?"

"I don't know, it's on this paper right here."

He hands me the paper when I look at it I see he's going to B-3 (The Animal House) That's were Black lives. How am I going to tell this nigga about Black?

"Yeah you in there with my nigga from Paris."

He stopped dead in his tracks. Looking at me like I had three heads.

"What the fuck you mean your nigga from Paris!"

"Look we're going to let that shit go! It ain't but me, you and Michael up here and they ain't got but a few so we riding together understand."

"Get the fuck out of here Dawg!"

"That's how it's going my nigga. The FEDS put me on some real homeboy time and these niggas just like us!"

"Look my nigga shit is still the same with me. So, if you say we bailing like this then that's what it is. But on my momma if this nigga gets out of line I'm going to split his mutha fucking wig you hear me!"

"I told you they just like us. That nigga said the something about you."

September 3, 2003
Happy Birthday to me

My 25th birthday and I'm so close to going home Got to make a couple of phone calls. I walk down the yard to the outside phones and to catch up with Bugz and Black. Now every since those two fools have meet you would think they were brothers. All they do is fuss and argue about a bunch of nothing. And I be damn as I'm going down the hill they were coming up the hill fussing about something.

"What's up ya'll?"

Black jumped straight to what they were fussing about. "Dawg tell this fool you go to the board on the 16th of April and not the 9th!"

"Why are you two dummies fussing about when I go to the board anyways?"

Before Black could answer Bugz let me know why they're in such a uproar.

"Man we bet two packs of smokes on it and plus this nigga thinks he knows everything!"

Now how do I get in the middle of this? These are my niggas so I dead the conversation ASAP.

"Come on I'm going to call Charlene I know she got something to say today my birthday."

As soon as I said that both them fools started smiling. Black knows Charlene like we do she used to live in Paris for years down on Horton Drive.

"She going to be talking shit today watch and see plus I bet both of ya'll she calls all us some little bitches."

So they stuck out their fist and I pounded both of them. Soon as we get to the phone those fools were arguing about something else. After a couple of rings one of my favorite girls in the world answered.

"What's up Beamer?"

"Happy birthday little bitch!"

"I told ya'll we would be a bitch."

They stopped fussing long enough to ask what she was talking about? By then Charlene could hear them so she took straight off talking shit like only she could do.

"I know that little bitch Bugz is right there so who's that other nigga all up in my business?"

"Black."

"You mean little Bill from Paris!"

"Yeah."

"Tell that little black bitch I said what's up?"

"I will both them fools just lost a pack of smokes a piece. I told them clowns you would call us some bitches before the conversation was over."

"Tell them I don't mean nothing by it ya'll know I love ya'll."

"We know baby but look what's going on out there?"

"Goldie's home; seen him running around all crazy!"

"When you see him again tell him we on our way."

"Will do love! Look ugly boy I got somebody sitting here all in my conversation so I'm a let them say a little something to you."

Before I could protest or say otherwise the other voice was on the line and it caught me by surprise.

"Hello, Telly!"

"Hello to you, Ms. Randi."

"How you doing?"

"Fine and you?"

"I'm fine, in nursing school and just living life."

"Yeah, that's good to hear."

We both got quite for a long minute. Shit was odd to me I ain't heard from her in years. So what was about to come next I would short stop it from the jump...

"Telly, I'm sorry for..."

"Hey, hey now! Before you start, it ain't called for. So keep that apology to yourself."

"Yeah, but."

"Look baby girl life is life. From this day forward, I'm a play it how it goes, no regrets and I'm all in on everything I do!"

"Well, I'm sorry anyways."

"Digg, well maybe I'll see you in a few months, maybe I won't. But either way, make sure you take care of yourself."

"You too, Telly. I love you!"

"Yeah, put Charlene back on the phone."

"Boy, you know better! Got this girl tearing up over your ugly ass!"

"Don't know why?"

"I know and you do to so stop playing hard, understand me!?"

"No letters, no money, no nothing! How I'm I suppose to forgive that?"

"Do you still think about her even when you shouldn't, love?"

"Yeah and that's the problem! See now I've seen things that make me demand loyalty. Without that, a person ain't shit in my book. Charlene baby, I've became a man on this one and my plans are to get rich! So anybody that's on my tracks when I get home and they're not part of my train, I'm running they ass over!"

"If you say so, nappy-head boy!"

"Look baby, the phone bout to cut off. You be sweet. I love you."

"Love you honey, baby, love!"

"Bye."

"Hold up boy, let me tell you something and you better not ever forget it understand! Don't never say bye to me, bye means forever so use I'll talk to you later or in a minute, understand me ugly boy!"

"Yeah, I understand baby. In a minute."

"Now, that's what I'm talking about. In a minute, love!"

I hung up the phone feeling good cause Charlene is the same all the time that's why I love her so much. What she said I would never let go. I won't never let nobody tell me bye unless I know it was for, forever. In a light weight day dream but was brought back to reality by these two _ fools arguing over who won the most ping-pong games last. DAMN I be glad when these niggas go up for parole.

"Fuck both ya'll lying so let's go to the gym and see who's the best is right now!"

"Yeah nigga you know it's 148!"

"You out yo mutha fucking mind nigga NOTSOB all day!"

"148!"

"NOTSOB fool!"

And this was how it was all the way to the gym but my mind was really elsewhere.

11-25-2003
My baby Charlene birthday and
De ja vu all over

I wonder if Charlene is up early this morning? When I was on the street the only way she would be up this early (7:30a.m.) was if she had been up all night drinking. Other than that, the sun would have to be gone down. Fuck it all, she can do is not answer or cuss me out. Hell the latter part would be normal. I picked up the phone and dialed her number.

"Hey love!"

"What you doing up so early, Beamer?"

"Why does it matter, you little bitch. You calling my house, remember!"

"Yeah, yeah. Well, Happy Birthday, baby!"

"Thanks little ole ugly boy! What you doing up so early yourself?"

Just thinking about it got me on edge. See in the pen and mediums, you had to be up before the doors pop open. Shit could go bad for you if you decide to sleep late. Minimum security no locked doors.

"Old habits die hard."

"Whatever boy. Where's them two other fools at?"

"I ain't seen them yet today."

"Telly I got to tell you something baby."

"Yeah well I'm listening."

"Found out I got cancer, love."

Stone cold silence cause my mind flashed back to Head-Bey. Did I hear her right? Maybe my hearing is fucked up.

"What you just say Charlene?"

"Boy ain't nothing wrong with your hearing! So don't be up there stressing you hear me!"

"Well, why in the hell did you tell me then!?"

"I know you ain't cussing at me you little bitch!"

"I'm sorry baby I didn't mean nothing by it."

"Don't be sorry you little red nigga be sharp! They're waiting on you to come home."

"Who is?"

"Everybody! Waiting to see what you're going to do. The only nigga out here eating is Pretty Toni!"

"That nigga been getting money since we were young."

"Well he's getting it all right now."

I got silence for a brief moment. My plans have just changed No since acting like no mark.

"He better make some room I'm on my way!"

"I know love but look I got all this food on the stove so you be good and call me back later."

"Nah baby, I'll call in a couple of weeks."

"Okay love, but don't be too long bout calling, you hear me Telly?"

"Yeah, I hear you. I love you Charlene!"

"You know I love you, little ole ugly boy!"

"Later baby!"

"In a minute love!"

CHAPTER 4

Damn can you believe it! My year finality made it around. I see the parole board in April I can't wait. Bugz, Black and Michael all go up the same day February 10. Hope all them clowns make it. I'm on my way to the gym to watch Black and Teezy play basketball but I got to call Charlene first. She most have been sitting by the phone cause she picked up on the first ring.

"What's up love?"

"Damn Beamer, what you knew I was calling or what?"

"Nah boy but the Lord answered my prayers today."

"What you talking bout?"

"Well Telly, they're going to do surgery on me tomorrow and I wanted to talk to you before I went in."

There was a long moment of silence. Now all my life as long as I could remember I've never, I mean never, heard my baby Charlene be quiet. And quite frankly it's scaring the shit out of me.

"All hell, you're going to be alright!"

She didn't give me a fast enough answer so I let something show that she always gets on me about.

"Well ain't you!"

"Who you hollering at boy! Ain't nothing wrong with my hearing I heard you the first time!"

"I didn't mean to holla."

"What I tell you about emotions?"

"That men don't deal in emotions so leave that shit to the ladies."

"I'm going to leave it in the Lord's hands so don't you worry bout me. I'll be here when you get home."

"That's all I wanted to hear."

"What's that black-ass Bugz doing?"

"Nothing. Crying about going home next month and getting on my nerves and Michael, too."

"Tell them bitches I said what's up love?"

"I will baby. Look Charlene, please don't you die on me."

"Shut up boy! You just make sure you're ready for the world cause believe me, all eyes will be on you, Telly LaMont Shyne!"

"They better get their sunglasses out cause I'm going to shine like the sun in July!"

"I know you are, love."

"I love you, Charlene Marie Jackson!"

"Love you, honey, baby, love!"

"I'll talk to you in a few days, baby."

"Alright love. In a minute!"

I put the phone back on the hook and made my way to the gym. After that call with Charlene, the rest of the night was a blur. That night I prayed and my prayer was for my momma and Charlene.. But, I doubled back and asked for a little something for myself.

"Lord, forgive me for what I'm about to do. I ask you now cause I won't have time when these hillbillies set me free."

Sleep wouldn't come that night but one thing was a sure bet It was my turn to be The King of my City.

February 1, 2004
That same sick feeling!

I woke up this morning feeling like I could run 20 miles. The closer I get to the board, the more excited I get. But I got to call Charlene she's been home since the surgery and I call ever other day. It's a lot of people waiting for the phone so I go to the gym and run on the tread mill. I bust out seven miles. Feeling good I jump in the workout with a few of my Blood homies. Afterward I race back to the unit to use the phone. Nobody was by the phone so I hurried up and dialed my number. After a couple of rings the line goes live but it wasn't Charlene it was Colette her daughter.

"Hey, boy."

The way she said it broke my heart into a million pieces. Feels like it's stuck in my throat no words came out my mouth.

"Dawg!"

"I'm here. What's up with you?"

"Nothing, but look baby, momma passed away this morning."

My luck got to be bad. She was my best friend, now all I got left is my moms. Lord please don't let nothing happen to her.

"Damn!"

"Calm down, boy. Momma talked about you last night. Said you would be calling today told me to tell you she loved you and to be good plus remember what ya'll talked about and the last part, Telly it broke my heart, too. Told me to make sure I told you goodbye."

Words can't explain how I feel right now My girl just told me goodbye. Now I knew without a doubt she was gone forever.

"Colette, I'm sorry. You know I loved me some Charlene."

"Yeah, I know and she loved her some little ole ugly Dawg, too."

"I won't lie. I'm fucked up right now. I'm so close to seeing the parole board."

"I know, she told me. But look, don't be stressing. She's in a better place, so stay focused on what you got to do, understand me."

"I will. But look, tell everybody I said hello. I love ya'll."

"I know, boy. We love you, too!"

"Take care."

"Alright baby. In a minute."

Damn, that sounded just like Charlene. I guess she got on everybody's ass about saying bye. I'm going to miss you something terrible. But I know you'll be watching along with Bell and ya'll going to smile at some of the things I do and ya'll going to frown at some of the things I do. Either way, the world better get ready because a untamed animal is on schedule to be released.

Later that day!!!!

On my way down the yard to get with Bugz and Black but first I got to call moms just to tell her I love her. I called no answer so I called right back, She picked up the second time.,

"Hey momma!"

"Hey baby how you doing?"

"I'm holding up what about you?"

"I'm fine just worried about you that's all."

"I'm cool but I can't lie momma it hurts just like when Bell died."

"I know you loved you some Charlene you and a lot of other people did too, but you got to stay on track and bring your butt home you hear me."

"I know I'm ready."

"You better be I don't want to see you up in there no more baby momma getting old."

"I hear you but look I'm about to go out and get some air I'll call home in a couple of days I love you."

"Alright baby, I love you and remember what I said stay on track please."

"Yes ma'am."

"Talk to you later."

After talking to moms, I walked straight to the gym. Black and Teezy got a basketball game so I'm a kick it with Bugz and Michael. Hope Bugz got some of that green I need to get right. Once to the gym I see Bugz and Snoody talking so I call them over.

"What's up ya'll?"

Bugz answered first. "Waiting on you so we can blaze!"

"Yeah Dawg, this nigga ain't doing nothing without you, Blood!"

"You shouldn't either after I saved your ass from those Victory Park niggas!"

"I know blood but damn I'm just trying to smoke something."

"Don't trip my nigga, we on our way."

I see my homeboy Michael so I call him over. "Mike, you going with us?"

"Hell nah, ya'll crazy as hell! Both ya'll about to see the parole board."

"What the fuck that got to do with anything?"

"Hold up, Dawg. Why you talking to me like that? I know you're upset about Charlene, but hell, that was my girl, too now, so be easy."

"You right, tell Black we went outside we'll be right back."

"Ya'll be careful out there."

"No doubt my nigga."

We went outside didn't take but a second. We smoked right by the gym door. We didn't care you talking about three young wild niggas who didn't give a fuck about nothing after we got done we went back in to watch the game. We sat at the top of the gym away from everybody else. Me, Bugz, Snoody and my nigga T-Dingy he's from Lexington. We watched the game Black'em won. Afterward I stayed back a minute so I could holla at Black.

"Look my nigga I ain't got shit when I get home."

"I told you the deal! My little brothers are waiting on me to touchdown. They got it jumping!"

"I need some of that in a major way my nigga!"

"Ain't no thang, baby juice. I got you!"

"That's what's up."

"Look though ya'll niggas smoked without me!"

"Don't worry about that we can fix that ASAP!"

Bugz and Teezy were standing not too far away from us.

So we caught up with them.

"Yo Bugz, help Black get his lungs out the street."

"Man, that nigga knew we were going to smoke anyways. He's always trying to get you to stamp something gets on my fucking nerves with that shit!"

"Well, make sure you get it done. Plus give me two so me and Teezy can get straight on are walk up the hill."

My nigga didn't hesitate. He handed me three so I'll let Teezy take one with him so Kapone could get straight in the unit. We talked for a couple of minutes then heard the yard re-call over the loud speaker. We shook up and me and Teezy bailed. Smoking, walking and talking Teezy unit is first (C-1).

"Be easy, blood. Tell Pone I see ya'll tomorrow."

"Will do, blood. Keep yo head up, shit going to be alright my nigga."

"I hope you're right."

Just as Teezy was walking in the door, I heard Kapone.

"Yo blood, it's a cold world, no mercy!"

I make the last 20 yards of my journey by myself with one thing on my mind. That's fucking that bitch! And the bitch I'm talking about is the streets.

April 16, 2004
The long wait is over!

Man I couldn't sleep last night. I see the parole board today. Freshly ironed suit, hair braided neatly to the back and my beard trimmed low. 12:30p.m. I grab my N/A certificate and headed out the front door of the unit. It's nice outside and niggas are all over the yard. Everybody knows when you're going up. Michael and Black made parole two months ago. Black already sent word to me said he'll be waiting. Bugz got a 13 month set back ain't nothing he can't handle. We had a talk last night that had me in my body.

"Damn my nigga I go up tomorrow I hope I make it!"

He doesn't say nothing at first so I look at him. What I see is something I've never seen before.

"What the fuck is your problem?"

"Dawg I know you're ready to go but I won't lie, I wish you were staying with me so we could go home at the same time."

"Are you out your mutha fucking mind!? Nigga when I was Terre Haute trying to stay alive I didn't wish you up there with me or when I was in Beckley nigga pushing my steel in niggas I didn't wish you up there and Lord let's not forget when I was 2500 miles from the fucking house in

Oregon with 1600 gang banger an. I was flying the mutha fucking Kentucky flag by my mutha fucking self! And would you believe it a nigga had the nerve to say he didn't even know there were black folks in Kentucky! So I had to bust his mutha fucking head on that statement alone, understand me!"

"Damn my nigga I didn't mean it like that!"

"Like hell you didn't! But I'm a tell you what you're going to do! You're going to lay yo ass down and keep yo mouth shut by the time you get home I'll have everything ready for us you hear?"

I didn't give him time to say shit! Now I'm on my way down the yard to the administration build. I see him and old Keg-Head they just shook their heads as I hit the steps two at a time. No time for games now these cracker got my life in their hands once again. Fuck it lets throw the dices hope I don't crap out again.

Later that day....

I called home and talked to moms. Now all I'm waiting on is my gold seal from Frankfort. I made parole told Bugz I'm leaving everything I can to him. Moms said Scoobie and my homie Moo-Coo would be to pick me up when it was time. Well world here I come, hope that nigga Black stands on his word.

CHAPTER 5

April 30, 2004
They open the gates and
all hell breaks loose!

I was standing in front of R&D at 6:30a.m. These crackers quick to lock a brother up, but slow-ass a mutha fucka letting us out. It was 8:30a.m. before I hopped in the car with my brother and Moo-Coo.

"Damn nigga we didn't think they were going to let your ass go!"

"Nah bruh, they can't hold this train no more, it just left the station."

My nigga Moo-Coo did the damndest thing. He ain't in the streets like most of my niggas but as I'm in the backseat putting on my clothes(all Polo from head to toe) he handed me a bank roll. This nigga got a wife and two kids I know he ain't hustling.

"My nigga you know I can't take this. You got your family to look after!"

"Nigga what you think I'm doing right now fool!"

"That's what's up my nigga!"

I do a fast count and it looks like bout a stack. Hell it wouldn't matter what it is was. In 48 hours I would be the man you had to see if you wanted to get your paper right. They take me to see my parole officer by the time we're done their phone are ringing off the hook. Everybody calling wanting to know when we're coming though. Hell I don't know why they ain't been checking for the Dawg. First person I want to see is moms.

When I do get to moms' house, I run though the front door. She was all smiles as we hugged.

"Let me look at you, baby!"

"I'm all here momma I'm fine."

"Momma going to have to fatting you up baby!"

"I know that right."

"Look baby, I know you're a man, but listening to what I got to say before you hit those streets. People in the streets don't care about you. I was the only one sending money and making those long trips to see you. So all I ask is for you to be careful understand me!"

"Yes ma'am."

"I ain't playing I'm tired of seeing you locked up!"

"Yes ma'am."

"Now come on I fixed some food you need to eat cause Lord knows when I'll see again!"

We sat down and ate Scoobie and Moo-Coo's phones must have rung 50 times a piece. They didn't answer them cause moms give them that look she wasn't in no rush to see me walk out that front door. After I got full I hugged momma and she whispered.

"Please be careful baby."

I squeezed her real tight cause I really didn't know when I would see her again. But one thing was for sure, I was about to sit the streets on mutha fucking fire.

New faces and old ones, too
but the same old hood!!!

Back in the car on our way to the hood, Moo-Coo puts in the little homies CD Goo and Marquis is really putting on for the town. By now I got a drink in my hand hell the Kentucky Derby is tomorrow. When we pulled up in the hood I see a red Caddy sitting on 24's and that bitch was clean. People everywhere all looking as we pulled up. Pretty Toni was the first nigga over to the car.

"What's up, bruh?"

We do a little shake and hug..

"Damn nigga, you fat-ass a mutha fucka!"

"I'm living, my nigga."

"I heard that looks like you living real good!"

I already knew the business, hell Charlene kept me up-to-date on the streets while I was away in school (ha ha ha). "I can't complain my nigga."

"Well, make room. I want to live some to my nigga."

"It's plenty room for everybody! Niggas just to scared and ain't got no plug."

Well little did he know I got a couple of plugs and the only thing I'm scared of is not having a place to hide all my money. After kicking it with him for a few more minutes he hands me a cell phone.

"Look my nigga it ain't much it's a pre-paid. Here a 100 dollar card to go with it."

"Good looking my nigga."

I slide all that in my back pocket didn't want people all in my business. I go holla at a couple more people then I see Snoop. I make my way over to where him and Rico were sitting. Rico jumps up and hugs me and started talking shit about how little I was.

"Damn nigga, I thought niggas got on swol when they go to the pen!"

I didn't hesitate for one second. I pulled my shirt over my head now I was standing there naked from the waist up. Most were looking on in amazement some were trying to read my tattoos. Either way, I was putting on a show.

"I'm in top shape my nigga don't get it fucked up!"

"You ain't bull shiting young nigga you cut up like Bruce Lee!"

We all laughed as I put my shirt back on. I walked over to Snoop and we hugged I felt him drop something heavy in my back pocket and no mistaking what it was. This was right on time cause I needed one anyways.

"I ain't got no bank roll for you but I know your bout to do you so here a little something to hold you over."

"Thanks my nigga you know I needed one anyways but digg what's going on out here?"

He threw his arms around my shoulder and we walked off so no one could hear what we were talking about.

"Look young nigga I ain't been in the game since you left for school. Pretty Toni got it on lock."

"I'm hip to that already my nigga."

"Well seem like you know all there is to know. Oh yeah, there's some niggas over in The Heights from Cincinnati getting a little money."

Little did he know Charlene had put me up on them niggas about three years ago. Damn them fools still here by the time I get done with them they'll wish they had took they ass back to The Queen City.

"Tru! Well I might as well tell you I'm about to get busy ASAP!"

"Didn't think you do anything else."

"You want some of this action that's about to take place?"

"Nah baby boy. I've been waiting on you to get home so me and TaTa can get married."

"Well what the hell are you waiting on!?"

"You so now the wait is over my best man just made it home from school."

"You better know the wait is over my nigga!"

When the sun
starts getting low!

I've been fucking with this stupid ass phone for a minute. Not paying attention to what going on around me I hear this little laugh. When I look up to my surprise I didn't know who she was..

"Is something funny?"

"Yeah there is!"

"Mind telling me what it is."

"You taking all day with that phone. Are you slow or something?"

Now I know this bitch didn't just pop slick out her mouth. Hell she don't even know me.

"What's your name anyway since you all in my business?"

"Del-Rae."

"Del-Rae! What kind of name is that?"

"The one my momma give me so let me help you with that phone!"

Damn baby mouth is slick but I could fix that with a little time. Plus her skin was this pretty honey red color. She fucked with my phone for a hot second then handed it back to me.

"You need to learn how to work your phone if you're going to have it!"

"This shit new to me. We wasn't fucking with this shit before I went away to school."

"Oh is that what you call prison?"

"Did I say prison? I said school!"

"Well people been talking about you for, let me see…I've been down here for two years, so I guess for 18 months, that's all I've been hearing. Telly this, Telly that. Well, I'm not that impressed by what I see."

"I'll tell you what stay around me long enough and I'll make you love me!"

A little smile crosses her lips I knew then we would be seeing a lot of each other.

"That's what your mouth says, you take care. Nice meeting you."

"You, too, be easy Redd."

"My name is Del-Rae!"

"I like Redd so that's what I'm going to call you."

"You're an asshole, you know that?"

"If I didn't know any better, I'd say you was white." With that she turned on her heels and started to leave but pulled up short and turned back around.

"Lose my number, please!"

"Hell I didn't even ask you for it!"

"It's in your phone! Oh I forgot, you're too stupid to know how to work it!"

I smiled cause I already got a soft spot for her. I waved and she gives me the middle finger. Now back to do what I was about to do. Call my nigga Black!!!!

Sunday May 2, 2004
Day after The Kentucky Derby!!

Most niggas would run straight home and get some pussy but hell how can a real nigga enjoy some pussy when you're broke. I talked to Black he said he would be to get me; didn't say when, said just be ready.

Sitting out, kicking it with some of the old homies, like Holla-Holla, Bo-Big Tony, Julio, Monte and a few others, I could hear somebody bass line dropping hard-ass a mutha fucka. Don't know who but they were hitting hard. I look down the street and see an all black Tahoe. When I say all black, I mean rims an all. I watch as it makes its way up the street I touch my back pocket to make sure my burner is where it belongs. The truck stops right in front of us me being the nigga that I am I ease close to the car I was standing next to. The bass wasn't hitting no more and my phone started ringing. I put my phone to my ear but never once took my eyes off that truck.

"Yeah!"

"Quit trying to look all hard baby juice!"

I couldn't do nothing but smile as the window on the truck came rolling down and Black was smiling and laughing with one of his homeboys.

"Nigga I liked to start pumping lead in that bitch while you playing!"

"Stop playing fool! You just got out I know you ain't got no thumper yet?"

I eased up next to the truck and pulled my shirt up just enough so he could see.

"Binky I told you this nigga was a nut case! Get in my nigga we're going to PKY!"

I hopped in the truck with Black and his homie Binky and we smashed out. When I get back to the town my turn to ball would be one to remember.

12:15a.m.
May 9, 2004

Man who of thought this I've been home a little over two weeks and my pockets are on swoll. Black give me two bricks and 10 pounds of weed I've been grinding non-stop ever since. Goldie's home and we're getting major money. Damn I'll be glad when Bugz gets out. Being in the streets nothing is safe not even your phone number. Randi been hitting me up and I really don't know what to do. I mean she left me for dead but hell the heart got a mind of its own. Snocp been telling me let's have some fun so tonight we hitting up Two Kegs. Man females all over and can you believe it I still ain't had no pussy.-

"Yo Snoop I like baby girl over there in all red." I was pointing at baby and she waved at me.

"Young nigga you only like her cause she's wearing all red."

"Nah she bought me a drink early so she choose."

"Man listen you just got out and that prison glow is all over your monkey ass. So you bout to have your way out here so just be careful understand me."

Just as I was about to go holla at baby girl I see Randi and her sisters. Hell half the hood was up in here. I don't know how I feel do I love her or hate her? Hell it really don't matter either way she fucks with some nigga from the Westside of Lexington. I'm a just play it how it goes. I go to the bar hell all this money in my pocket and it's burning a hole in it. So I need to spend some of it.

"Excuse me ma'am I'm buying drinks for all the young ladies standing here."

Shay-Shay, Shan, Crytal, Kitty, Kay and a few other. Shan say to me...

"Thanks Dawg!"

"They don't call me that no more."

"Well what the hell the calling you then boy?"

"Topp Dawg."

"Topp Dawg!"

"Yeah with two P's for a double dose of this mutha fucking pimping!"

Damn I don't know where that just came from, but I know Pretty Pie would've loved to have heard me spit my shit.

She just walked off laughing with her silly self.

2:45 a.m.
The Waffle House!

Feeling good and hungry me and Snoop was already at the spot. This fool was doing 100 mph all the way home. Me like a big dummy was cheering him on with a brand new .45 in my back pocket. Fuck it I'll rather get caught with it then without it. But right now, we've got food all over the table and we're talking shit.

"Young nigga, you get some pussy yet?"

I hung my head a little cause I was about to tell a lie, "Nah, not yet."

"What! You mean to tell me you ain't got yo nuts out of pawn yet?"

"Look my nigga I was broke when I got home! How was I suppose to enjoy some pussy when I couldn't even feed her afterward?"

"I guess you got a point! My young nigga is growing up."

I got my back to the door and Snoop stopped talking. So out of habit, I touch my hip just to make sure my thumper was where it belonged.

Snoop whispered, "Here comes Randi and everybody that was at the club."

I keep on eating cause it was about to get hot up in here. Shan and Kitty made their way in our booth. Shan, like a nigga, reaches on my plate.

"Mmm boy this good I'm so hungry!"

"Keep yo nasty hands off my plate! Go order you something an I'll pay for it."

"All this food on this table, hell I'm going to eat with ya'll plus it takes too long!"

"If I was still in the pen I would go upside yo black nigga head!"

"Well nigga you ain't in the pen no more, plus I would beat yo little ass!"

All I could do was smile. She was going to talk shit with the best of them. After a few minutes of kicking it I told everybody their food was on me. Kitty leaned over the table and told Shan.

"Let's go find another seat. I see somebody trying to get next to that red nigga sitting right there."

"Yeah let's do, that so my girl can get at her man!"

I almost choked to death when she said that. Hell I ain't nobody nigga yet! Snoop started smiling and rose straight up and went with them to another booth. My wait wasn't long cause she slide right in the booth with me.

That same school girl smile still makes my heart soft for her.

"Hey baby girl how's it going?"

"Fine Telly! Why you been dodging since you've been home?"

"Can I be honest with you?"

"Please do!"

"You wasn't checking for me when these cracker where sending my ass all over the country so why now?"

"I was scared and didn't know how to handle the situation."

"Couldn't have been more scared then me! Plus I could've showed you how to handle the situation if you would've stayed around!"

"Look I don't want to argue."

"Well, what do you want from me then!?"

Damn I was a little too loud. Charlene would be on my ass about not keeping my emotions in check So I lean a little closer to her.

"Well, I'm waiting?"

"I'm I going with you tonight?"

"Yeah I guess you are."

Everybody was sitting around kicking it and enjoying themselves. Me and Snoop had stepped outside.

"I'm going with Randi my nigga."

"You're grown my nigga so do what you want. Hell she's good people cut her some slack."

I looked at that nigga like he had three heads. Hell he don't know the feeling of someone leaving you for dead when you need them the most. I play it cool cause he would say the something that Charlene would say about emotions.

"I guess you right hell I'm a little nervous about getting some pussy."

"It's like riding a bike my nigga you never forget."

"Here she comes, I'm out bruh."

"Have fun tonight Dawg and tomorrow play it how it goes."

"Show you right fam."

"You ready, baby?"

"Yeah, let's bail."

We got in her ride and smashed out it was the wee hours of the morning. Hell I didn't know what was going to become of this but right now I'm on my way to handle my business.

Back to the streets
Full steam ahead!!!!!!!!

I can't lie last night with Randi was fun But I got to watch my heart. On the way to drop me at my mom's we're kicking it about a little of this and a little of that. My phone rang an I didn't look at the caller I.D. screen cause if I had I would've never answered the call marked private.

"Yeah!"

"Yo is Randi with you?"

Talking about being caught flat footed. Her nigga calling my phone.

"Nah I don't know where yo girl at!"

Now she's looking all stupid cause she knows dude is on the phone. This nigga is having a real sucka attack. So I nipped it in the bud.

"Looking pimping I don't know how you got my number and I don't care but don't call my phone looking for yo girl when you can't find her!"

I hung up and turned my attention straight to Randi. "How the fuck he get my number!?"

"I don't know I'm sorry!"

"You might be in a little trouble when you make it home."

"I'm saying something to him soon as I get there!"

"Nah, play it cool."

"I'm sorry, Telly, really!"

"Don't sweat it."

Deep in my own thoughts so when we pulled up in front of moms house I didn't even notice.

"We're here, Telly."

I didn't say shit. I hopped straight out the car and didn't look back. I made my mind up right then and there. wasn't no room for her in my life right now. The hustle is all I got room for so nothing else matter.

Later on that day

I've been asleep all day but. I smelled food cooking so I jumped straight up moms was smiling at me.

"This the first time I've seen you since you got out."

"I know baby I'm sorry."

"Ain't nothing baby you just be safe."

"Yes ma'am."

"You got some mail on the counter."

I see a letter from Bugz but it got Luther Luckett Correctional Complex on it. Damn I wonder what the hell he done got into now!!!

"Momma can you drop me in the hood later?"

"Yeah baby let me know when you're ready."

We sat down and ate I hopped in the shower and got dressed. Moms dropped me in the hood at my Uncle Stiks' house, and Uncle Pee-Wee lived next door so I was safe here. All the work is here Unk don't even stay here much got a white girl in Cynthiana he be laid up with. His son stays here and by the way things look I'm a be staying here too. Turtle goes to school every morning and Uncle Stiks be gone at night so shop was wide open. I'm bagging up the work and Goldie's phone is ringing like crazy. I can't count the number of times that nigga run out the front door. Once he came back we had a few minutes to kick it.

"Goldie you stacking yo paper my nigga?"

"Yeah fam shit got real sweet since you came home and put half the hood on."

"I can digg it my nigga But check this out we got to get to the tattoo shop tomorrow got something I want to do. This wild ass white boy from Seattle put me on this one!"

"Dawg what the hell you talking about now?"

"You'll see but peep this we got to send Bugz some money ASAP!"

"Yeah let's do that tomorrow."

"Find Kay and let her do it."

"Okay but let's cook up the rest of the work so it'll be ready!"

"Fuck it, let's get busy!"

I've got to be out my mutha fucking mind. We're about to cook up 2 keys of cocaine. I just left the FEDS where niggas got all day for far less then I already got cooked up (534g) that going to get us a life sentence in any courtroom. By the time I get done whipping all this work I would have plenty extras off the top. My young nigga Volume showed me the whip game and I swear to God it's proper.

Late May 2004...

Me, Parker and Mailman were standing on the front side getting a little paper and this little red car zooms up the street with somebody in it that I been meaning see. So I holla...

"Don't be shy stop and give a real nigga a few seconds of your time!"

Them two fools started laughing. Mailman spoke up... "Quit hollaring my nigga they see you."

I guess he's right so we keep hustling and a few minutes later she came back...

"Damn Nicole you that busy you can't stop and give me a few seconds?"

"Nah just looking for somebody that's all."

"The looks over you found me!"

That got a smile out of her. Time to go to press mode. "Look, here's my number, use it when you get some free time."

"Okay I just might do that."

With that I watched her pull off into the fading day light.

A few days went by and I still hadn't heard from Nicole. Fuck it my hustle comes before anything anyways. Posted up getting paper that won't fold I turn to look across the park and I see that little red car with a bunch of females standing all around it and they were all looking my way. Only one had my attention so I made my way over there. The closer I get the more and more Nicole was acting like a shy school girl. They all got real quiet as soon as I got there.

"Hello, ladies!"

All of them speak at once but I was looking dead at her. That smile has me trapped so I put my business out there in front of everybody.

"Damn beautiful. I give you my number and you didn't even use it. What? I ain't yo type of nigga?"

"Nah, you my type, I just lost it, that's all."

Now I may look a little crazy but I know she didn't lose it so I put the full court press down one last time.

"Look I'm a give it to you again but don't take it if you ain't going to use it."

Before she could say anything Kiki jumps right in her business.

"Telly, I told that bitch to call you!"

"That's alright she'll call when she ready for a real nigga in her life."

I turned and left them with their mouths hanging open. I know she'll be calling real soon now back to my mission getting money. Standing on the front side Colette came through on her way to the liquor store So I sent my money to get something to sip on. Just kicking it make money time is of no essence. I look up and my phone started ringing. I liked not to answer it because I didn't know the number and you know how that can be (ha ha ha) but curiosity got the best of me and I'm glad I did answer it.

"Yeah!"

"Dang that's how you answer the phone?"

"It's mine ain't it?"

The line got real quiet so I spoke up first.

"Hey baby, don't trip off me what's on your mind?"

"Nothing just calling to see what you were doing?"

"Come pick me up and find out!"

"Give me a few and I'll be through."

"I'm on the front side."

"I know somebody told me they just saw you out there posted like a light post."

I smile cause that was the truth if I ever heard it. This paper chase is all I know right now.

"Digg I'll be waiting."

"Alright."

Damn near a hour had went by and she still hasn't showed up. I started to call her back but why she said she was coming so I'll leave it at that. Still trapping with my back to the street Holla-Holla says something I've been waiting to hear.

"Who's this little chocolate cutie waiting on?"

I turned around to see who he was talking about an a smile crept across my face.

"I'm out Holla you be safe out here."

"Nah young nigga you be safe!"

He was laughing as I walked over to the car and got in. I could tell she was a little nervous so I did my best to make her feel comfortable around me.

"Damn baby, I didn't think you were coming."

"Nah I had to handle a little business that's all."

"I can digg it so what you want to do?"

"I don't care as long as I'm with you."

"Okay let's get a room and chill then."

"I'm with that."

So we rode out making small talk on the way. Once to the hotel I went in and got the best room they had. Hot tub, a king size bed and mirrors every mutha fucking where. I got a fifth of Crown Royal so me being the nigga I am I drink straight out the bottle like a cowboy. Once I wetted my whistle I started running water in the hot tub.

"Here baby, take a drank and try to relax. I won't bite you unless you ask me too!"

I got a little smile out of that but I watched her take a drink and she surprised the hell out of me.

"Hey, be easy. Wouldn't want you to do something you wouldn't want to do if you weren't a little tipsy, ya digg?"

"Oh, don't you worry. I intend to do everything on my mind since the first day I saw you out!"

"I ain't got a problem with none of that!"

"I didn't think you would."

Fuck it time to show off a little. I took my shirt off and when I turned around she was just stirring at me with her mouth wide open.

"What's wrong baby?"

"Nothing, but damn!"

Now for those of you who don't know being in prison makes the body a piece of artwork if you work at it. Plus I got tatts all over my body and my nipples are pierced. Yeah that was the wild shit I was talking about going to get done. She walked straight over to me all that nervous shit was out the window. She rubbed my six-pack and licked my shoulder at the same time. After that she looked me straight in my eyes and I knew then she would be in my life for a long time.

"Slow down love, I ain't going nowhere."

"Damn, you sexy as hell!"

Now that made me smile cause I ain't never had a female say no shit like that to me. I put my pistol on the nightstand so it would be within my reach.

"Let's get in the hot tub for awhile."

"Hell yeah! Let's do that, daddy!"

She never took her eyes off me as we both got undressed.

We got in and I was sipping out the bottle talking about a bunch of nothing but I couldn't keep my eyes of those big chocolate titties floating in the water. I looked her in the eyes and no words were exchanged as she slid right up in my lap. She started licking my ear and from there she stared biting my neck I don't know when she did it but I was in the pussy. The way she was squeezing it had me short of breath in that hot tub. Her hands were all over my body, made me think she had ten hands she was enjoying herself and made me feel good. But what she said in my ear was more then I could handle.

"Damn daddy, this dick feels sooo good!"

Hearing that shit made me stand straight up out the water with her still wrapped around me. She had the funniest look on her face when I done that. I had to be careful in that water. I didn't want to break both our necks showing off. She bit me real light on my shoulder so I sat her down real easy like.

"Let's go in the bedroom so I can show you I'm a big girl for real!"

"Lead the way baby. I'm right behind you!"

We got out of the hot tub and she wrapped up in a towel. Me, being an animal, I say, "Fuck a towel!"

I followed her to the bedroom, butt-ass naked with the drink in my hand. I jump right in the bed, wet and all.

"Oh shit, I forgot my gun in the front!"

I jumped straight up and went and got my gun. Pussy always got a nigga slipping that way; a lot of real niggas dead to this day.

She just shook her head when I ran back in the room and hopped right back in the bed. She was just watching me licking her pretty lips.

"Come get me baby!"

She dropped her towel and crawled right between my legs. No time was wasted, she put me right in her mouth. I tried to get away from her but to no avail. So I took my treatment like a big boy.

"Damn baby that shit feels good!"

"Mmmmmmmm!"

Now all real niggas know good head has a way of making niggas turn into a freak or in my case waiting to see how far a broad will go. Having fun is having fun, so let's get this mutha fucking party popping!"

"Come here baby, let me lick that pussy!"

She rose up off the dick long enough to smile a kool-aid smile. We 69'd for a while. Now, I had to get back in that pussy ASAP.

"Let me hit it from the back, baby?"

She doesn't stop sucking on me right away but she stopped long enough to say, "Let me ride this dick first baby."

"Do you baby. I'll get mine later."

She got up on the dick and damn that pussy was good. She bounced and rolled until she busted all over me. I didn't waste one second not to even let her catch her breath. I flipped her on all four and I went to smashing that pussy like no other. Now mind you, I've only been home couple of months and yeah I've had a little pussy and shit, but my hustle comes before anything. But now I see something I plan on keeping so I put in some major work.

"Damn daddy, you feel so good!"

Now why she go and say that? Now I really got to make her mine. But little did I know she already was. I stood strong in that pussy for ten minutes but that was a major task to hold off that long! So I got to my breaking point.

"Damn baby, I'm cumming!"

"Cum wherever you want to, daddy!"

Me being a nigga, I don't pull out. I cum all in her. Damn, we took a short break, the next thing I know, the sun was coming up and we were still at it. So, we called it quits for now I'm a hustla so it was time to hit the block.

"Look here baby you can stay until check out at 12:00p.m. but I got to bail."

"Nah baby I'll drop you wherever you need to go. I'll just go on home."

"Look baby, you cool? I don't want you to think I'm hitting and running it's just my job comes first."

"I know who you are and I'm cool cause I got what I wanted too!"

On the ride to the hood we made plans to see each other real soon. She works 3rd shift at the Toyota plant. We pulled up in the hood and Holla-Holla and Monte were sitting on the bench drinking beers already. I looked at her, no words were exchanged; none was needed She kissed me on the cheek and whispered, "Please be safe baby."

I didn't say shit cause what I might've said would've been too much for the first night. Little did I know she felt the same way. Holla-Holla's eyes lite straight up on sight. When I heard that famous saying as soon as I stepped out the car I knew then today would bring a real nice bank roll.

"Whoop! Give me a wake up my nigga I'm working for you today!"

CHAPTER - 6

Early June
Just the person I need to see....

Man, me and Nicole been hanging out every weekend I'm digging her so I make time on the weekend. Now I need to get some wheels of my own. I got all this paper put up an it's time to shine a little bit plus Snoop's wedding is coming up. But today my luck changed for the better. I run into somebody I've been meaning to catch up with and now I'm replaying the conversation over in my head.

"Yo bro!"

I was standing in the line at the Super America. Hearing that stupid-ass white boy voice put a smile on my face. I turned around and was looking death in the face.

"Damn Ant, what's up?"

Hell I could already tell what's up but this was my man so it's whatever when it-comes to him.

"I heard you were out!"

"Yeah I've been home for about two months. What's going on with the family?"

"Man Dad's in the car business now you really should go see him."

Just earlier today I was thinking about some wheels and what do you know.

"Yeah man without a doubt."

There was a long moment of silence I could tell he wanted to ask me something but didn't know how to go about it. So I lighting the situation for him.

"Ant man, what you on?"

"Nothing heavy bro, just enjoying life, that's all."

"Look here's my number use it understand but don't wear it out, ya digg?"

"Hell bro thanks I'll be seeing you soon."

We parted ways but my dude looked real bad. That crack shit is fucking him up. Still day dreaming my brother Scoobie and my family J.D. were hollaing at me.

"Damn boy wake up! You want some ice in your cup?"

"Yeah fam you zoned out you ain't in the pen no more so come on back to us!"

"Yeah put some ice in the cup for me I'm going in the Learning Center to use the bathroom."

I holla at the nigga Terry who runs the place I heard his little brother is getting money up in Cynthiana I'm a have to check on that. On my way back out I see someone who I've been trying to get at. So I put a little pep in my step.

"Aye, aye you I know you hear me!"

"Yeah I hear you but my name ain't aye either!"

"I'm sorry Redd can I have I moment of your time?"

"I told you my name nigga either use it or don't say shit to me understand!"

"Del-Rae let me get in your ear for a second."

I really want to get in her panties but her ear a do for right now.

"Where you been I tried to get at you?"

Little did I know she had a dude But hell what do I care it's all about me now.

"I've been busy so what did you really want?"

"Nothing just trying to see what's up with you?"

"Nothing and that's all you wanted to know?"

"Not really wanted to know if you wanted to kick it or something?"

A little smile crossed her lips now she's on my level and that's always a good thing.

"Yeah that would be cool."

"What about tonight?"

"Nah tonight wouldn't be good but I'll call you though you take care."

"Yeah you do the same. Oh by the way you don't have my number!"

"Yes I do! Did you forget I programmed your phone?" She rolled her eyes like I irritated her. Baby's mouth and actions need to be toned down but that's okay cause I'll get her in the long run.

"Well use it then!"

"When I get some time I will thank you very much!"

With that she walked off. Fuck it right now anyways I'm kicking it with my brother and family right now. Hell she probably feels it in her bones anyways I'm going to make her love me like her life depends on it.

Later that night

Sitting on the front side faded like a mutha fucka. Scoobie J.D., D-Mack, Rico, Snoop, Monte, Goldie (that nigga is on the run for a parole violation),Disco and a few other were shooting dice under the shelter. I was sitting on the bench next to the street. Work was moving slow so I closed my shop down hell all the young niggas where out trying to get their bank up. That put a smile on my face cause ain't nothing better than seeing a young nigga on the grind! Smiling enjoying the sights my phone rings.

"Yeah!"

"Damn you a rude nigga!"

"Well hello Miss Redd!"

"Where you at?"

Talking about sobering up real mutha fucking quick! I've been robbing and jacking since I was a young nigga so I paid close attention to what came out her mouth next.

"Why?"

"I need to ask you something that's why?"

"I'm listening."

"Nah I want to see your face when I ask you this!"

What the fuck could she want that she got to see my face?

"I'm on the front."

"Okay I'm on my way."

I flip my phone shut and walked over to my brother's truck. I reach inside and grabbed my pistol shit ain't going to go like she thinks if shit's funky you can bet that. I watch this car pull up and so does everybody else. The window came down an it's was her I walked over to the car with my hand on my gun.

"Yeah baby what's on your mind that you got to see me face to face?"

"Can I go with you tonight?"

The look on my face must have been what she wanted to see cause she laughed at me.

"Well!"

I didn't say shit I walked around the car and got in. Once the door was closed, she turned up that Lil Boosie "Show yo tat's."

Shit was slamming and show my tat's I would do.

> Showing my tat's and
> About to steal another heart!

Moms was gone to Texas to see my Uncle. He some big time lawyer for some potato chip company. So I took Redd to moms

I had to watch the house. Once in my room I put on some music but I guess it wasn't to her liking cause she was looking at me like I was crazy.

"I got a CD in the car that might be good."

So we walked back out to her ride. After getting her CD, she reached in the ash tray and grabbed a blunt. Man, she's out her mutha fucking mind to think she's about to smoke that shit up in moms spot. She must have read my mind cause she put some fire on it right there. She didn't offer me none. Hell, I was fresh out I wasn't going back for no dirty like I seen a bunch of other suckas do. She hit it four or five times then put it back. We made our way back in the house and she put her CD in and turned off the light and got naked. I wanted to see her but she put up one helluva protest.

"No leave the lights off please!"

Since it was our first time together, I give her that one. But see there is a street light next to my bedroom window so I opened the blinds. DAMN! She had the world's meanest tan lines; I'm talking mean.

"Damn baby, you sexy as hell! Why you didn't want me to see all this?"

"Cause I'm shy, that's why!"

I take my shirt off and when I had it up over my head I heard her make a funny little gasping sound. Shirt all the way off and she was smiling but her eyes land on my nipple rings. She uses her finger to tell me to come over to her once close enough she says.

"Damn, I like this!"

She licked my nipples then my six-pack. I stepped back and jumped out of my shorts and boxers as fast as I could. I crawled right between her legs. Kissing, biting, touching; shit's getting hot real mutha fucking fast but she stopped me.

"You got any rubbers?"

"Damn. You bullshitting, right?"

"Nah nigga, I ain't. Hold on!" She pushed me off her and went in her pants pocket and pulled out three rubbers.

Damn I can't remember the last time I wore one of these. Fuck it if thats the only way I'm getting in this pussy, so be it. She crawled right back to where I was between her legs and went right back to what we were doing before are short beak. I felt her grab my dick and slip the rubber on. The next thing I knew I was in that pussy she whispered in my ear.

"Pull my hair, baby; please!"

Man that pussy was so hot and tight I lost my mind. Pulling on her hair and sliding in an out that pussy, she pulled her legs back so I could stand up in that pussy. Acting a plum fool having an absolute ball while doing so.

"Baby I'm going to cum on you!"

"It'll be my pleasure baby if you do!"

She started shaking and locking her legs all around me. Now you know, my waist is little but I swear it felt like she was made just for me. I let her get herself together then I tell her.

"Turn over baby and let me hit it from the back."

Man those tan lines were killing me. I look down at that ass and I notice the rubber had busted. Thinking out loud got me caught.

"Damn!"

"What's wrong, baby!"

"Nothing!"

She must have felt me cause she turn around with another damn rubber in her hand.

"Come on!"

"Put it on or we're finished!"

I slid it on and went back to smashing and she trying to run.

"Where you going, baby?"

"Mmmm. Mmmm, you feel so good I'm going to cum on you again baby!"

I don't say shit. I keep smashing once I seen her shaking I grip her hips and pull her all the way up on this dick.

"Oooh shit!"

I smile. She just let me know I put in some major work.

"Turn back over baby."

As she turns back over, me being a nigga, I snatch the rubber off.

"Put it back in for me, baby."

She grabs my dick now she feels that I don't have the rubber on.

"Just like a hard headed nigga!"

After that statement she slid me right up in that pussy.

"Oh my God!"

"What? You can't handle this hot pussy without a rubber on or what nigga!"

"I thought you were shy?"

She threw her legs up on my shoulders.

"I was, but you bring something out of me. Now, fuck this pussy baby!"

I have fun for about five more minutes.

"Oh shit baby!"

"You better pull it out!"

I pulled out and busted all over her stomach She acted like she had acid all over her.

"Get a towel and hurry up and get it off of me!"

I took my time going to the bathroom. I could hear her bitching all the while. I like baby even her fly-ass mouth. I get her straight then fall back up in the bed with her. She got right up in my arms and went straight to sleep. I threw my arms around her and dosed off myself.

Look at the wheels!!!!

I ain't heard from Redd since she bailed that next morning.

Hell she ain't even answering her phone. Fuck it. I'll catch her on the rebound. On my way to Big Ant's car lot to see what I can get. As we pull up I see some real nice rides that already has my attention. Once inside, a couple of sales reps try to get my attention but I want to talk the big man. After about ten minutes he came walking out the back with a big ass smile on his face. I stood to shake his hand but he grabbed me in a big ass bear hug that had everybody looking at us.

"Hey son how you doing?"

"I'm fine Big Ant!"

"Hell boy you look a little on the thin side!"

"I'm cool but I need to talk to you about a car."

When I said that Big Ant wrapped his arms around me and we headed to the back. Once we were in his office it took a few minutes before he said anything.

"Look Telly you are your own man so I won't preach but I will ask you one favor? Please don't sell that shit too Anthony please!"

"I won't Big Ant I promise."

Hell Ant's my main man so I'll just give it to him. That way I can keep my promise of not selling it to him.

"Thanks son! So what you trying to drive off the lot?"

"That Yukon Denali!"

He does a soft whistle but I guess he don't know I'm strapped with cash. All this money on me got me looking like the state puff marshmallow man.

"Do you know how much that cost, son?"

I didn't say shit I stood up and started pulling out stack after stack of money and throwing it on his desk.

"Son, all I want you to do is give yourself a winning chance. So I extend my home to you if you ever need to get rid of a problem. Lord knows I don't want to see you back in that fucking cage!"

"Thanks Big Ant, I might need that."

"Don't you mention it. Now let's get you rolling son!"

After we did some paper work that makes it look like I'm making payments but I really paid cash up front I pulled out the lot on my way to get some more work.

Late June 2004
Snoop's wedding night

For a present to my nigga I took him shopping. I brought him some light pink Mauri gator to match his suit which was light gray with a light pink tie and vest. Me I'm going in all red with white pin stripes, two-tone red and white Mauri gator with a matching belt. As I'm getting dressed, moms comes in my room.

"Hey baby you look good!"

"Thanks."

"Telly I need you to slow down just a little bit, okay."

"Okay so don't be stressing."

"Can't help it your my baby so I'll always worry about you."

"I'm going to be okay momma."

"Alright baby I love you."

"Love you too!"

As soon as she walked out I grabbed my shoulder rig that Mr. Saint gave me that holds two pistol and rushed to put it on. I got to put this hot ass suit jacket on so she won't see them as I'm leaving the house. Fuck it that it's damn near 90 degrees. Her heart means more to me than anything so I'll make do until I make it to the truck. I know she's going to want a kiss so I got to catch her sitting down so she won't try to hug me. I took a few more minutes to get fly soon as I step out my room I catch her sitting on the couch watching TV I rush over and kiss her on the cheek and jump straight out the front door. Once in my truck I turn the AC up sky-high and put my nigga Lil Boosie in my ears.

"Girl, give that pussy!"

Tonight I would be getting all I wanted and some. Just a few months ago I was in prison but now I'm on my way to the top.

Party time...

This a hood wedding so me and Jim-Bob were the bar tenders at the reception. Snoop set it out too. All you .could eat and drink on him. Once we were sit up I took my jacket off and boy was that a big mistake. Jim-Bob just smiled but I got a ear full from Colette.

"Boy you know better didn't you just get out!"

"Don't start Cool Water damn!"

"Nah somebody needs to say something to your young wild ass!"

"Okay so you said it now what?"

"Take'em off and I mean it!"

I just look at her but she wasn't budging one inch. So I pull my 9mm and my .45 and put them under my suit jacket by now my nigga Snoop had made his way over to the bar.

"Snoop Cool Water is tripping!"

"Nah he's the one tripping got his guns all out in the open for everybody to see!"

As soon as Colette said that Snoop unbutton his jacket and eased it open to revile he was strapped to.

"See I ain't the only one!"

"Yeah but he ain't fresh out of prison either little boy!"

If she don't sound just like my baby Charlene.

"I love you, Cool Water!"

"Shut up boy and fix my damn drink you and this black Jim-Bob make me sick!"

Hell, Jim-Bob didn't have nothing to do with it but he just smiled and blow her a kiss. So with that I hurried up and fixed her two drinks so she wouldn't be in no rush to get back to the bar. She got her drinks and walked off shaking her head with the party getting into full swing. People everywhere dancing, eating, drinking I mean having a funky good time. I see some of the home girls and they looking good, smelling good but all that just got put on the back burner. What I'm looking for just walked in the door. Damn Nicole was looking good to me! The bar was so thick she couldn't get to the front so I fixed her and Kiki a drink and told Bob.

"I'll be right back my nigga."

"Hold up pimping!"

I turned around to see what he was talking about and can believe this my nigga was handing me my pistols and suit jacket.

"I don't want you caught way over there without your thumpers my nigga."

"Sho you right blood!"

Damn that the first time I've used that since I've been home. But that's what he was to me the love he just showed me is love from Blood. He smiled but I handed him my jacket back but put my guns were they belong. Fuck it niggas know how I get down anyway so they going to play it close. On my way across the room I could feel all eyes on me but I don't know why hell this is my dude's day to shine. I finally make it to where Nicole and Kiki were sitting once there I hand them their drinks and I leaned straight in and Nicole kisses me right on my lips.

"You going with me tonight?"

"Hell, yeah! What you think I was going to let you go with one of these other bitches? I don't think so you're the only reason I came!"

"Dig that! It's me and you when the party's over."

"Say that then baby."

Kiki was just smiling but she couldn't let me get away without saying something.

"Boy you look damn good!"

"Thanks baby if ya'll what something else to drink get my attention and I'll bring it to ya'll."

On my way back to the bar I was getting mad dogged by a few females but that shit don't hold no weight hell I call the shot around this bitch. As the party went on to the wee hours Anthony Hamilton song "Charlene" came on. I walked over and got Nicole we about to leave anyways so why not dance with my lady. With my suit jacket on and her with her purse on her shoulder we started dancing. She pulled herself up real tight but stepped straight back away from me. She opened my suit jacket and pulled both pistols out and them in her purse. Damn with every passing second she was stealing my heart. Now back in my arms so tight I could feel her heart beat baby don't know yet but she just became my new favorite girl in my life. After the song I go holla at Snoop.

"Congratulations big homie!"

"Thanks baby boy!"

"Look I'm about to be out, you staight?"

"Yeah young nigga. Go enjoy yo'self. I'll get at you later."

"NOTSOB!"

"Without a mutha fucking doubt, my nigga. NOTSOB all day!"

So, with that, I walked over to Nicole and grabbed her hand and walked out the door into the bright stars of this beautiful summer night without a care in the world for now.

Kash'd Out

CHAPTER - 7

Can you believe it? Shit is going real smooth, money is piling but I know it could be more. Those Cincinnati niggas over in The Heights gots to go. See they're less than an hour's drive from home so with them just to the north of us and Lexington to the south I'm about to tighten shit up around here. This is my city and I'm about to let everybody know it. I call Goldie that nigga is still on the run but I know he's down.

"What's up my nigga?"

"Laying down until the sun drops."

"Look we got some business to handle."

"True, I'm in got to get straight before my luck runs out anyway."

"I'm a hit you later, be in all black."

All I heard him say before I hung up.

"Lights out creep slow move silent."

He was already on point but I'm a call one more nigga and take his wild ass with us. I know he's with whatever to make a dollar, plus he's like me hates out of town niggas trying to make a dollar in are town that nigga Disco will do just fine.

I sent Holla-Holla over to The Heights to see what's up and to get a position on them fools!

"Dawg they posted up in that white bitch B.J.'s spot."

"Good looking what I owe you family?"

"It ain't nothing baby boy wish I could put in a little work with ya'll."

When I really took a look at the old nigga I seen a real O.G. He been putting in work since the late 60's so I kept him alive with what I said next.

"Man you just did! Hell you put us on them niggas so you put us in play."

"Yeah young'un but ain't nothing like that pistol play!"

"I can digg it my nigga but look take this half and lay low for the night I'll get with you later."

"Yo Dawg don't leave nobody alive in that house if shit goes bad you hear me!"

I didn't say shit as I pulled off Goldie and Disco was getting high as a mutha fucka. I found a spot to park but not to close when I turned and looked at those two fools I knew one thing for sure. Death will be visiting somebody tonight.

"Look ya'll these niggas was strapped so don't be playing when we get up in here!"

Both them niggas to geeked to say shit. Disco got a 12 gauge Roit pump, Goldie got two 9mm's with extended clips on them. Pulling down our ski masks I mumbled really to myself, didn't think I said it loud enough for them to hear.

"Take no prisoners."

Just as light as I had said that both them niggas say. "Leave none alive."

One thing I did know the Scott County coroner was going to be very busy tonight. Outside the front door we could hear them in there talking shit.

"Yeah, these country ass niggas is easy!"

"Sho is. I can't believe these niggas let us open up shop in they city!"

"Told you they were some bitches!"

94

I looked at Disco that niggas nostrils flared up so big you could drive a Mack truck through them. I throw up a finger to tell him to wait but it was too late. Damn that nigga pulled a straight kick door we caught them two niggas drinking and smoking.

"Bitch nigga shit ain't easy now! Get yo mutha fucking hands were I can see them!"

Both them niggas tried to touch the ceiling in this bitch they sho ain't talking that shit right now.

"Where's that bitch at?"

Neither one of them niggas answered my question fast enough so Goldie pumped one in the nigga sitting closest to him. After that we heard the toilet flush with the music playing a little loud that bitch most didn't hear shit or thought it came from the song. Either way Disco hit the steps running two at a time and came back dragging that bitch like a cave man. It took all I had in me not to laugh when he kicked her dead in her ass.

"Bitch, get yo funky ass over there!"

Once she was seated on the couch next to the other nigga she looked down and seen dude on the floor bleeding she knew then shit was all so serious.

"The dope is in the freezer please don't hurt me!"

I thought to myself to late for that as I watched Goldie bail straight to the kitchen. He came back with all the work. "Where is the money at, nigga?"

"Fuck you, pussy niggas. I ain't saying shit!"

Before I could say anything Disco blow his whole head off his shoulders. Like Holla-Holla said don't leave nobody alive Goldie shot that bitch up and I leaned right over dude on the floor and put one in his head.

"Leave a little of that work out so the police can find it and hurry up!"

We had five minutes tops to do what we had to do. On the way out the backdoor I looked on top of the ice box as were leaving and see something out of place. A box of fruity pebbles laying flat while the rest of the cereal was standing up. I know these stupid mutha fuckas didn't! So I grabbed it and could tell right away it wasn't cereal. BINGO!!!

August 29, 2004
Let's Celebrate!!

Man can you believe it that bitch made it after getting hit six times. She couldn't give the police much cause we were masked up but she's talking a little too much for me. Goldie got picked up on a parole warrant so me and Disco were doing are everyday routine. Today is a special day though its Nicole's birthday hell I don't know what to get her, but I knew it was me and her tonight. Right now me and Snoop were on our way to the mall.

"Dawg why in the hell did ya'll leave that bitch alive over there?"

I didn't say shit hell I didn't even tell this nigga we did that shit but everybody knows we done it but couldn't prove it one way or the other.

"Look I know you three niggas can handle yourselfs, but never leave anything to chance, understand me!?"

"I'll get with her on the first opportunity that presents its self that's for show."

"You do that my nigga. When Bugz coming home?"

"Maybe March or April I ain't for sure."

"Well, whenever he gets here, make sure that bitch comes up missing with her face on a milk carton, ya digg?"

"That's as good as done."

Later that night...

I'm fresh in my standards if you ask me. Black t-shirt, polo jean shorts and black Chuck Taylor's with big red laces. I've been dressing like this ever since I've been home. I get all kinds of looks from different people especially when I'm in Lexington those Westside niggas be mad dogging but what do I care. They ass better be ready to go all the way cause I won't be coming up short when it come to my life. Right now I'm on my way to pick up Nicole and Lil Boosie and Webbie was jumping as I pulled up out front. Before I could call her to tell her I was out front she was coming out the door. Baby was in all black with red open toe heels real mutha fucking sexy. I hop out the truck to be the gentlemen I really am.

"Damn baby you look real nice!"

She kissed me right on the lips and smiled that sweet smile that I like to see.

"Thanks baby you don't look to bad yourself."

I get her in the truck and we pull off heading for the straight for the interstate. I got her some good smoke but I won't be hitting it to fresh out the joint.

"So what you want to do baby?"

"I don't care as long as I'm with you nothing even matter I've been waiting all week to see you."

"I ain't mad hell I've been waiting to see you too."

"Baby, where's your gun at I know you got it?"

"Under my seat, why?"

"Give it to me just in case we get pulled over."

See that's why she's my woman and don't even know it yet. That's more than once she rode with my pistol in her position. I slid her the gun and she put it straight in her purse. After we hit the city (Lexington), I took her to eat. As we're sitting down, eating, she says the damndest thing.

"I love you, boy!"

I almost spit my drink everywhere. We've been kicking it hard since the first time we hooked up hell she's my girl even though some people don't like it but their opinion don't count in my love life. I never responded to what she said and it didn't seem to bother her one bit.

"Baby, will you take me to get a tattoo?"

"It's your birthday. I'll get you whatever you want!"

I had bought her a diamond necklace but I ain't give it to her yet. I'll wait to later. After eating, we went to the Tattoo Charlie's on New Circle Road. Before we went in I give her the present I got for her.

"Happy Birthday, baby!"

She didn't even open it. She jumped right in my lap. Kissing and grinding all on me like her life depended on it.

"Hold up, baby! We got all night for that and as many more nights and days for you to give me all that loving, understand?"

"I know but you just make me feel some kind of way when I'm around you, that's all."

"I can digg it baby, but let's go in here and get your tattoo and after that I'll give you all of me you can stand."

"Okay baby, I'm trying to over-dose on you tonight."

"We better keep the paramedics on standby then!"

We walked in the shop laughing. She looked around for a hot minute but not long cause the next thing I knew she was in the chair getting worked on. I just looked around the store because I'm already covered in tattoo's no room for any more. Time most have gotten away from me because the next thing I know, she's hollering for me.

"Baby, come here and look!"

I guess I wasn't moving fast enough so she started hollering again.

"Telly, do you hear me!?"

"Yeah baby, I'm right here. Now let me see what your working with!"

She spun around in the chair an all I could do was smile. She put my government name on her titty.

"Damn baby, that's how you feel?"

"Hell yeah boy. I'm all yours!"

Now I'm the one that steals a kiss but not just any kiss but one you share with someone when shit's about to get hot and heated. The tattoo dude cleared his throat with a smile on his face.

"That'll be sixty bucks and get a room!"

"My bad, today's her birthday."

"In that case, her tat is forty."

"Thanks."

I paid for the tat and we bounced. Now, time for that all night love session I promise her and I intend for this be the best gift of the day.

Sept 2, 2004
One I'll never forget!!!!!

Tomorrow is my birthday with me and Nicole birthday so close I got to get some extra fun out the way tonight. I got a rental car but no where's to go. Me and Snoop started drinking real early that Crown Royal and coke had a nigga on fire.

"Damn young nigga what we going to do?"

"I don't give a fuck my nigga I've missed so many b-days locked up I'm just happy to be free for this one!"

"I hear you my nigga but let's go to the strip club or something."

"It's whatevea my nigga long as the fun don't stop."

So we sit a time to go but right now half the hood was out having a good time enjoying the weather. A few hours had gone by and the sun had long been out the sky. Just as we were about to go to the club my phone rang.

"Yeah!"

"Damn baby juice, what's up?"

"You know, bout to hit the city!"

"Fuck that, bring yo ass down here!"

"Say no more my nigga we're on our way!"

"We out on Sterns."

"Nigga, I know!"

"Hurry up Shawn-T said he's going to drink you under the table!"

"Tell that nigga Notsob is on the way to the 148!"

I could hear that nigga talking shit as I was hanging up my phone. This would be one for the record books.

Notsob and 148
The party that won't stop!!

I let Snoop drive to Paris, hell I was already twisted. When we pull up there were cars all up and down the street. We get to the door and Black's stupid ass got to hollering.

"The mayor of Georgetown is here!"

"You know what it is my nigga!"

"What you got in that cup?"

"Just a little Crown, that's all."

"Nigga pour that shit out all we drink down this mutha fucka is Grey Gosse!"

We finality make it in the house and it was standing room only. Niggas everywhere Whoodie, Two, Horatio, Big Crutch, Binky, Shawn-T, Colt D and a few other. Snoop and Horatio went straight to smoking that purp. Me I looked straight at Shawn-T.

"Nigga, here I go!"

"Took yo country ass long enough tc get down here! Let's go in the kitchen so I can show you how we get cown!"

Can you believe a nigga from Paris calling me country this nigga on some real groovy shit already guess I'll try some of what he's having.

"Nigga lead the mutha fucking way this yo city!"

Once in the kitchen I found out one thing. If the police kick this door in nobody I mean nobody will ever get out of prison again. Hell damn near everybody in the house is on parole. Two with his slick ass got shit popping.

"What ya'll nigga going to do?"

"Set something out so I can treat myself."

With all the drink, weed and white girl I could do in front of me the party was on and popping. I holla for Snoop him and Ratio came walking to the back plus Big Crutch was behind them with the video camera. Me and Shawn-T went shot for shot and blow for blow.

"Nigga 148!"

"You out yo mutha fucking mind Notsob all day fool!"

We went at it like this for damn near an hour straight. Everybody was laughing and shaking their heads. Snoop had gone back up front a long time ago I know this nigga is white boy wasted so I make my way up there.

"My nigga, you straight?"

"Hell nah! I'm fucked up you and them young niggas in there is wild ass a mutha fucka!"

"Shit's fun my nigga. I've been in that cage for so long all I want to do is party for those real niggas that's never come home again you feel me!"

Just as Snoop was about to say something when Horatio walks in with a hand full of purp Snoop starts shaking his head before Ratio even said anything. I think he already know what was coming next.

"Snoop, roll this shit up! Dawg we taking yo ass to the 730 Club then we going to the city to the strip club!"

"Nigga, hell yeah! I'm with all that!"

Snoop starts talking to Ratio. "Fuck that ya'll taking me to Georgetown first!"

"Hell nah nigga, you going with us!"

"I can't lil brother I just got married I got to get home before the sun comes up you feel me?"

"I can digg it but at least go to the 730 with us then Dawg and Tony will take you home."

"After that I'm done ya'll some cool young niggas for showing my lil nigga love like this."

"Tony loves that nigga so I do, too. Now roll this kill so we can blow it before we leave!"

We hit the club downtown Paris and shit was cool. Me and Black stood in the middle of the dance floor killing shot after shot of Grey Gosse. I know everybody thought we were crazy standing face to face seeing who would fold first.

After that, we followed Snoop back to Georgetown. Once there, me and Black hopped out the car.

"Snoop, you have any fun tonight?"

"Nigga what! You young niggas is America nightmare! Young black and don't give a fuck! All I ask is you keep this one out of trouble we need him."

"I got him you sure you don't want to come with us we bout to act a fool!"

"Nah I've had enough you young niggas be safe."

"Later bruh, we out!"

Me and Black hopped back in the ride and smashed out. I look at the clock on the dashboard and it read 12:51a.m. It's officially my birthday. Damn I ain't seen one of these free in years. I know what Pusha would say.

"Shit don't stop til the casket drops!"

And I would party for three straight days. But one thing loomed in the back of my mind and that's calling California.

Christmas Season 2004
The five bricks and a door key!

I'm sitting at moms with the number T-Banks had giving me in my hand. Fuck it I'm about to use it to see what's really going on out west. I dial the number and it rings four or five before some lady picks it up.

"Hello."

"Hello may I speak with T-Banks."

"May I ask who's calling please?"

"Dawg I mean Telly ma'am."

"I know who you are by either baby. You're the little country boy from Kentucky that he's been waiting on to call. So you finality decide to call well you just sit by that phone and somebody will be getting with you soon as possible."

"Yes ma'am."

"The boys said you had plenty of manners."

She hung up after that so I just sat around doing nothing flipping though the stations while mom ran around cooking and 'cleaning. Not paying attention to the time the phone rang I looked at the caller I.D. box and the same number I had just called was calling back.

"Hello."

"What's up country nigga!"

Man I ain't heard this nigga voice in a minute but T-Banks was on the line.

"I can't call it shit's slow down here Damu!"

"I heard that! Look Big Tone asked me every time he calls had your country ass called yet and when I say no that fool sounds disappointed."

"Tell that nigga I'm cool just checking to see what the weather's like out there."

"Can you believe it the snow stays falling in sunny California?"

After that statement he let out a little laugh.

"Can I ski O.G. or what?"

"I told you from the jump not to use this number unless you wanted to get paid. You already know you were on soon as you dialed this number so stall me out with that bullshit!"

"That's what's up Blood!"

"Look the homies are posted up down in Pine-Bluff Arkansas they the closes ones to you so give me a couple of days and when your ski's land they are 14.5 but only when you're done. Five pairs are on their way but one is free cause it's the holidays."

"I'll be waiting!"

"Look Blood you on count so you owe me one understand?"

"Anything Damu just say it, and it's as good as done."

"I'm a hold you to that, lil homie."

"You do that, but you be safe blood."

"Yo Dawg, remember it's a cold world. Blood no mercy!"

"Until the mutha fucking world blows up!"

Christmas Eve 2004

The birds landed and I dropped the price around here by 200 dollars. Niggas is hot but what the fuck do I care when I was doing time. Them niggas were doing fine. I've been posted at Uncle Stiks house grinding non-stop I wasn't turning anything back. If they only had five dollars I had some crumbs for them. Hustla or smoker the price was the same. Me and Turtle was sitting around playing Madden when a horn blew. Turtle jumps up and goes and look to see who it is.

"Fam, it's Nicole."

I get up and go to the door. All though my truck is parked next door everybody knows that I'm in here. I open the door and just stand there.

"Come here baby!"

"What am I going to get if I do?"

"Me!"

As I step one foot out the door I turned right back around. I left my gun on the table hell that's too far to be without it. So I finality make it to the car.

"Yeah baby."

"Since its Christmas Eve, I want you to stay with me."

"Hell baby I thought I already was. I got the room so that's a done deal."

"No room tonight baby, my place."

I just look at her I've never been in her spot hell we always go to the room. But I look a little closer and I see love all in her face.

"It's whatever baby!"

"Here take this."

I look at what she was giving me and I knew then she was officially my girl. A door key was in her hand.

"You sure baby?"

"Yeah that way you can let yourself in whenever you want."

I leaned in the window and kissed her real soft on her lips and Kiki just giggled.

"I'll see you tonight baby!"

"I can't wait either!"

"Look do me a favor have nothing but your high heels and the radio."

"And my necklace you give me for my birthday."

She pulled off laughing as soon as she turned the corner the God Father came around the other corner and pulled up before I could get in the house.

"What's up young nigga can a pimp get a Christmas deal on the hard or what?"

"I'm feeling good O.G. what you got?"

"A stack!"

"Nigga, since it's the holiday, I'm a give you two zones for your money!"

"Damn young nigga, I don't know what these other niggas is thankful for but I'm thankful yo young ass is out the pen. Damn Christmas is going to be good for everybody this year!"

"Just happy to be home for this one my nigga that's all."

"I know that's right young soulja!"

We walked in the house laughing and talking plenty shit.

Later that night

I had Turtle drop me off at Nicole's. I didn't want everybody to know where I was at even though she lived on the Hillside with the white folks I still had to be careful. I make my way to the front door I could hear music coming from the apartment. I ease the key in the lock and ease my way inside with my pistol in my hand. Shit looked nice in here candles burning music playing hell I just sat down on the couch with my gun under my jacket. I waited to see what was coming next.

"Take your coat off baby and relax!"

I don't know how she knew I was in this apartment shit beats the hell out of me. I easy my jacket off but I still had my gun in my hand. On my momma anybody but her walk out that back I'm killing them and her. Still waiting to see her and the wait was well worth it if I must say so myself.

This chocolate mutha fucka walked out the back butt-ass naked with some black open toe heels on and that damn necklace I got her for birthday. I couldn't do nothing but smile at her and she walked over and jumped straight in my lap.

"Ouch, baby!"

"Sorry!"

I pull my pistol out from under her and she just shook her head at me with a smile.

"Damn baby you smell so good!"

She didn't say shit, she bit me real hard on my neck and I know that's going to leave mark.

"Ooooh shit, baby!"

"Baby, take us to the back!"

Without a moment's hesitate she wrapped herself around me and I stood straight up with her. But hell I ain't leaving my gun out here so I look at her and she reaches down and grabs it for me.

"I love you, Nicole!"

When I said that, tears formed in her eyes.

"I love you, baby!"

I could hear Pretty Pie now.

"Love ain't nothing but a misunderstanding between two fools!"

What do I care, hell this is my first Christmas home and things couldn't be better. Only thing missing is my nigga but I can feel he's on his way.

April 2005
Time to put in some work!!

The last time the work landed so did this phone. The nigga who brought the work down this time his name was Spookey.

"Dawg what's popping Blood?"

"Stacking paper and staying out of one time face."

"That what it is Blood but digg this. Banks said to keep this phone close to you and never use it. It's for him and him only so when it rings answer it don't feel like you're the only one with one cause we all have one."

He pulled the phone from his pocket and it looks just like the one he just give me.

"I hear you my nigga."

"Look I brought six this time I'm going back home(Cali) for awhile so this ought to hold you until Killa T makes the trip 30 days from now."

"Tell Killa I said to bring some X pills when he comes."

"Nigga you tell him you got his number just like I do!"

"Yeah you right. Be safe on your long journey to the beautiful land!"

"Look out Pasadena here I come and I've been missing you!"

That was two months ago. Sitting around counting money with Uncle Pee-Wee drinking his early morning Miller's High Life talking shit my phone rings. I reach for it.

"Yeah!"

"Yeah!"

But it wasn't my phone I use every day it was the other phone T-Banks had sent to me. Uncle Pee-Wee just shook his head as he killed his second beer of the morning. It had stop ringing by the time I had got it out my pocket.

"Shit boy how many damn phones do you need?"

"This is the bat line. Uck hell, this the first time I ever heard it ring my damn self."

But as soon as I sat it on the table so I could catch it if it started ringing again it cranked right back up.

"Yeah!"

"What it B like Blood!?"

"Money piling, hoes smiling and all the junkies speed dialing that's what it B like!"

"Young nigga you hung around Pretty Fie to damn much! You're starting to sound like that nigga! But that good your money is piling that all I ever want to hear from my family."

"Yeah but what's up? I know you didn't call to talk about how I'm handling my business down here. Hell I know Spookey, Killa-T or Ms. Lady keeps you posted on that so quit stalling me out!"

"Damn lil homie you all business, huh? Well, time to earn your flag the right way!"

"Already did that, my nigga!"

"Nah homie, the real way you feel me! So be at the Louisville

International Airport in two hours got a first class flight on Southwest waiting on you."

"I'll be there, Blood!"

"I got a little female up there that has everything handled, so don't worry about nothing. I got you soon as you land.

I didn't say shit else as I hung up the phone. I called my brother Scoobie so he could take me to Louisville to catch my flight. I didn't say much on the ride but that nigga was asking a lot of questions about why I was getting dropped off in the city. So to smooth this niggas nerves over I give him some rap.

"Bruh, look I got something to do so do me one okay? If something happens and I don't make it back home there's a shoe box in my closet at moms with a $180,000 in it make sure she gets it okay!"

"Look I don't give a fuck what you're going to do! Just go do it and bring your ass home understand!"

We hugged and I turned and headed for gate 5. Next stop for this country boy was sunny Southern California.

CHAPTER - 8

The out of town shooter

The flight out west was cool. Hell this the first time I've been on a plane without handcuffs and shackles on. I was at the world famous Los Angeles International Airport (LAX). I was just now getting my one bag and had my back turn to the oncoming traffic so I never saw who was standing behind me.

"What's up, Cuz!?"

My mutha fucking ears turned beet red. Damn do I stand out like that? Fuck it shit about to get real mutha fucking ugly! Soon as I turned around with my fists balled up ready to go to war I was looking dead at Pusha, Spookey and Killa-T. Them niggas were dressed like some C.E.O. of a Fortune 500 company.

"What the fuck you niggas doing tripping like that!?"

Pusha was the first to speak.

"Nah Blood you the one tripping! This L.A. fool or did you forget where your country ass is at? Hell the way you dressed you would think it's 88' again. You lucky yo wig ain't laying on this mutha fucking pavement!"

Let me tell you what I got on. A red Polo t-shirt, black Polo pants and red Chuck Taylor's with big red laces in'em. These fools got on all black and it ain't no Polo. All top of the line shit like Prada, Gucci and some shit I can't even pronounce.

"Fuck it Blood, I'm doing me!"

Now Spookey was the one about to start talking my head off with his bullshit. Hell every time I see him or Killa-T their dressed just like I am right now.

"Yeah Damu shit's cool but at home we dress like this so one time can't tell the difference between us and all the movie stars or athlete. Look at Killa his monkey ass looks like he might play for the Lakers or the bum ass Clippers!"

"Well now I know so ya'll going to take me to get some of what ya'll got on or what?"

"Hell yeah we got you! Let's bail Blood we got people waiting on you anyways."

We smash out in a big boy 600 SEL I'm talking a mutha fucking space ship. I didn't ask where we were going cause I had feeling anyway Bingo! Pasadena was our destination. They bail straight through the hood Killa-T give me a light weight tour of their hood.

"This Lincoln Avenue Blood."

No more was needed to be said That was all these niggas talked about in the pen was their stomping grounds. Now I see it firsthand. We keep it moving and rode past the Rose Bowl on to some real beautiful home that look like they cost a arm an a leg. The driveway was full of big boy rides same shit you see on the rap videos. We hop out the ride and Pusha went back to the same shit from the airport.

"Dawg T-Banks is going to be hot with you about what you got on so be ready."

"How the fuck was I suppose to know! Hell that nigga called and said get to the fucking airport so I did and this is what the fuck I had on so stall me out blood damn!"

"In the future please dress appropriately when your country ass flies out here okay!"

"Yeah, yeah nigga whatever."

We walk in the house and shit was laid out. I could hear voices as we were making are way through the house. Once to this big ass day room I see Banks but the nigga standing next to him was my nigga On-One. But everybody was just looking at me like I was crazy or something. Just like the homies who came and got me from the airport they too were dressed like business men. T-Banks walked over to me with a funny look on his face.

"Blood I'm going to say this just once understand. Don't ever dress like this when I send for you understand me?"

"Yeah Blood I understand but I didn't know all I did was get to the airport like you said."

"Don't sweat it! Now you know One will take your country ass shopping when we get done here."

"I can digg it my nigga."

"Well come on I want you to meet the rest of the family."

I already knew On-One, Pusha, Spookey, Ms. Lady and Tiny Tim. Now I meet his other two brothers. The Professor and this nigga is a real college professor at Cal State Berkeley up in The Bay Area. Then his little brother who is his lawyer his name is Tony a.k.a. T-Shot. Then T. Banks main man Byrd Dogg. He's half black half Samoan 6'5 320 pounds of all muscles. Him and One are Banks' personal security. They all showed me love like I was one of them since day one. As we were sitting kicking it the phone rang and everybody got real quiet as Banks answered the phone.

"Hello! Yeah, his country ass is here."

Now I wonder what the fuck is going on as Banks walks over and hands me the phone?

"Hello!"

"What popping, lil blood!?"

Well I be damn! Big Tone was on the phone.

"I can't call it, Damu! How you doing?"

"I'm fine now since your country ass came on it out the cold!"

"Look my nigga I'm forever grateful to you for putting me down so anything I can do let me know."

"That's why you're sitting there with my family now. Your one of us but

113

it's something we can't do at the time so it's all on you lil homie."

"Say no more O.G. it's as good as done!"

"Damu, Love lil homie. Put Banks back on the phone."

"Be easy, Blood!"

I handed the phone back to Banks and nobody said shit as him and Tone Finished their conversation. Once done I got my mission and instructions. I was going to Malibu to kill this nigga who had fucked up 200 bricks. Me and On-One but I was to be the shooter and he was my insurance.

"Blood, we counting on you!"

"That count is good then my nigga!"

"Now somebody take this country ass nigga shopping!"

Everybody laughed but I was in my own little world. I was about to put my murder game down 2500 miles from home. That's a long mutha fucking way from Kentucky.

No way out and my
Flight back home

I've been out here for two days. Nicole has been blowing my phone up non-stop but how and the hell do I tell her I'm in Cali about to murk a nigga? Tonight's the night soon as I'm done their putting me on plane home. It's sit up to where I'm this clown ass niggas limo driver got to pick him up at 8:00p.m. and my flight leaves at 9:30p.m. On-One is to follow me in the pickup car. It's 7:50p.m. and I'm sitting outside this niggas house. Talking about nice! Too bad when that nigga walks out the house it's his last time ever seeing it. Damn here comes this mark and he got a bitch with him! Too mutha fucking bad she got to go right along with this nigga! I get out and open the door for them.

"Good evening sir, Good evening ma'am."

This mark ass nigga just turned his nose up like a bitch! Now I know I was going to have fun killing this nigga. I shut the door after them and as

I'm going back around to the driver's side I look down the long-ass driveway and I could see One throwing up the set. I smile cause this nigga is super stupid to be banging at a time like this. I get in and let the petition down.

"Where to, sir?"

I caught this nigga with his hand up ole girl dress. Better hurry up and try to get his rocks off cause shit is coming to a end real fast.

"Don't you got a fucking phone up there with you!?"

"Sorry sir this is my first time."

"I'm going to tell Bill on your stupid ass, you can bet that!"

The 9mm with the silencer on it was sitting on the seat next to me within easy reach.

"Now take me to Miz Wong on Figueroa and hurry the fuck up, I got reservations!"

"Right away sir, but I got a message for you."

"What kind of fucking message you got for me!?"

This nigga is trying to be hard in front of this bitch! And she sitting there with a stupid ass smirk on her face like dude a straight killer or something. Shit's going to be fun killing her uppity ass, too.

"My big homie T-Banks said your debt is paid in full!"

"What the!"

That was as far as he got before I pumped two in his head. The bitch started screaming and had her mouth wide open so I put one right in it and blow the back of her head smooth off. I hopped out the limo and On-One pulled straight up.

"Shit done, blood?"

"Yeah I put that mark to sleep and that bitch too!"

"Hold up my nigga, got to get something from that nigga!" One jumped back in the car and came out a few second later with a small axe.

"What the fuck you about to do with that!?"

"Banks said he wanted this bitch-ass niggas' pinky ring!"

"Well take the mutha fucka off his finger then!"

"Hell nah! I'm taking his whole mutha fucking hand!"

"Just hurry the fuck up, nigga!"

That nigga jumped in the back of the limo and I could hear him talking to himself more or less than he was talking to me.

"Awww shit, Blood. You blow this bitch's brains out."

Shit is fucking amazing this fool was laughing to his self.

About twenty seconds later, he hopped back out the limo covered in blood holding this niggas whole hand.

"Damn Blood, you handled yo business up in that bitch!"

"Nigga let's go! I see why they call you On-One cause nigga you sho on On-One."

We jumped in the car and smashed out in the beautiful west coast setting sun. My body count just went to four. That nigga I killed trying to rob Snoop several years back, that nigga over in The Heights and now these two. I knew one thing was for sure, I could kill again without batting an eye. Sitting at the airport with T. Banks, Byrd Dogg and On-One waiting for my flight to depart, Banks was kicking his bo-bo.

"Dawg, you down lil homie so anything you need, let me know."

"Just keep sending that work O.G. and I'll be fine."

"All day, Blood!"

"I might need a little extra when my nigga Bugz touches down."

116

"Whatever you can handle down there I will send it without hesitation."

Right then over the loud speaker my ride was called.

"Flight 502 from Los Angeles to Louisville is now boarding at gate 9."

"That's my ride O.G."

"I see why Tone was crazy about your country-ass, you all business."

They walk me to the gate then On-One asks "When you coming back, Blood?"

"Whenever Banks sends for me."

"Next time bring Bugz with you, he sounds like my type nigga."

"Oh, believe me, you two niggas are just alike!"

We shook up and hugged I didn't look back hell I could feel it in my bones I'll be seeing plenty of L.A. in my future.

> May 2, 2005
> Kentucky Derby weekend
> time to ball til you fall!

Man I'm going to Louisville tonight! Going to get with my nigga I met in the state joint. Real smooth nigga name Frosty Dogg and he's from The Eastside and they flying that RED flag. I give Nicole some money and said well met at home base at 3 or 4a.m.

"Baby you sure it's cool for you to be dressed like that going to the city?"

I wanted to say bitch I just left L.A. dressed like this I can go any mutha fucking where I want like this! I got on all black with red laces in my Chuck's and my red belt I got at the swap met up on Crenshaw when I was in Cali. But I don't cause that my baby being worried about me.

"Yeah baby shit's cool I'm going to The Eastside it's like Pasadena all Bloods!"

"Well make sure you take that big ole gun in the closet that wrapped up in that beach towel."

She's talking about that AR-15 Killa-T give me the last time all the work landed.

"Nah baby I'm cool my nigga got me plus that .44 bulldog a make a nigga get right."

She smiled a nervous smile but I didn't tell her I was taking my lil nigga Ty with me. My young nigga lives down stairs just got home from boys camp might as well take him with me he's going to be a gangsta anyways.

"Just please be careful baby and make it back home to me!"

"You just be here when I get here, ya digg."

With a quick kiss I jumped out the front door and my young nigga was sitting on the steps waiting for me. He was in all black with red and black J's on the #11 all I do is smile cause the young nigga is down.

"What's popping, Blood!?"

"You know, big homie! B's popping and C's dropping!"

I smiled cause Killa-T and Spookey would've loved to heard this young nigga popping P's and crossing his T's. Damn T-Banks was right I think and sound like Pretty Pie more and more every day. Fuck it pimping ain't dead a lot of them hoes is misguided and undecided and need just a little direction that's all. (Free game to the few sucka who might pick this book up).

"You put those thumpers in the truck?"

"Yeah, they in there."

I had Ty put the 12gauge Roit pump and the mini-14 in the truck couldn't have Nicole all in my business.

"You ready to bail?"

"I'm with you Blood!"

"Let's get there then my nigga is waiting on us."

Inside the heart of
The Derby City

We make it to Louisville in 45 minutes. I hit my nigga Frosty Dogg on his cell.

"My nigga where you want me at?"

"Ain't but one place my nigga Shepherd Square on front of the Stop & Shop!"

He give me directions to The Eastside once there, I see his truck. A two tone white and green Yukon on 24's. When I pulled up everybody had on red and black I mean everybody.

"What's it B like?"

"You got it, Blood!"

"I know that's right but who's this young nigga you got with you?"

"This my young shooter Ty, he's wit it."

"Oh yeah, what's up lil homie?"

"Ain't nothing, Blood."

"I like him already Dawg so look lets go park your truck at my old lady's house cause ya'll riding wit us."

I meet some of the niggas with him some real laid back niggas that look like they could go from 0 to 60 real fast when the time calls for it. Head and Block fired up the purp on sight with my lil nigga Ty and he went straight in with them. My thing is them X pills but I'll get them later. Once we parked my truck, I whispered to Frost Dogg, "Do we need these?"

I showed him the shotgun and the mini-14 and that nigga looked at me like I had three heads.

"Dawg you niggas crazy fo real! Ya'll rode all the way up here with that!?"

"Hell yeah, nigga! The war can start anytime, anyplace!"

"Nah, you won't be needing that tonight. The white flag is up all over the city everybody is out to have a good time tonight."

"Okay if you say so but I'm keeping my pistol and my nigga is too."

"I knew you had one of those hell I got mines too!"

"Let's get my stuff so I can have it in the truck so I can smash out soon as we get back."

"What you trying to get?"

"A gallon of syrup and 500 x pills."

"Damn nigga you bout to get fucked up down there!"

"You worring about the wrong thing, my nigga."

He just smiled at that so we handle that part of business now to the party part. Ty looked mad cause we had to leave all the big artillery behind. First stop Billy's down on 26th and Broadway! Shit was on super swoll. First thing out my nigga Frosty Dogg's mouth when we got.

"Remember what I said the white flag is up tonight."

No sooner had he said that a whole pack of niggas came mobbing past his truck and all them nigga had on blue.

"Them niggas from Victory Park."

I just bit my tongue this was their city I'm just guess. Man the females were everywhere with a little or next to nothing on. Ty's eyes and tongue were hanging all out his head. I smile cause I feel good to see my nigga having a good time.

"Damn young nigga tighten up back there."

"Dawg all these mutha fuckas is nice!"

120

I let him do him. Hell he was telling the truth though they were real nice to look at. We hung there for a minute then we smashed out. On are way down 7th and Broadway going past Fats the strip joint the strippers were outside. They wasn't naked but wasn't much on them either. They had the grill out people just having a good time even myself I had a ball. I look up it's 3:00 a.m. bout time to be making it to home base.

"Look my nigga we got to B making it home before people get to worried about us."

"I can digg it, my nigga it. B like that."

"Thanks for the good time Blood."

"Ain't no thang baby boy, anytime."

After taking me to get my truck he showed us how to get back to the expressway so we could get home. Ty was hyped up out his fucking mind.

"Damn Blood that shit was live!"

"It was cool Blood now calm the fuck down for a second!"

"My bad just ain't never been to the city like that and get to have fun."

"I feel you my nigga but fix us a drink and cut up that Lil Boosie blood!"

Hell I couldn't tell him I felt the same way when I was L.A. only difference was I was on a murder mission and not for a good time. My train of thought was broking when my phone started to vibrate in my pocket.

"Yeah!"

"Well hello stranger!"

I almost crashed my mutha fucking truck! Redd was on the phone. I had seen her little sister Mel about a month ago and asked about her. My number had changed so I ask her to pass it to her. Now here she is at 3:30a.m. in the morning on my phone.

"Damn I thought you forgot about nigga!"

"Nah just tying up some loose ends, that's all."

Really, her and dude ain't seeing eye-to-eye. Too bad for him cause once I get my hooks in her she mines.

"Ty cut it down blood I can't hear!"

"Oh you got company with you I'll holla at you some other time okay."

"Nah that's my young'un he knows how to mind his own business."

"Okay, don't want to get you in any trouble that's all."

So we kick it until I pulled up in the apartment complex. We agreed to see each other real soon On my way up the steps Ty say to me.

"Dawg I'm down to do whatevea my nigga!"

"I know you would blood or I wouldn't have took you with me tonight."

I walked in the front door straight to the back bedroom. It was so dark I couldn't see shit had me feeling for my pistol. "Bout time baby now come get in this pussy!"

"It's the only place I want to be right now anyway."

"I know that's right baby!"

May 23 2005
They turn a wild ass animal loose!

My nigga Bugz made parole yesterday. Today he'll be home an all I got for him is a brand new 9mm with an extended clip. He'll have to make his own bank roll cause I got plenty work here too. I was at Uncle Stiks house posted up waiting and Turtle was talking my ear off with that foolishness.

"Dawg ya'll niggas ain't been out on the streets together in years!"

I was thinking to myself how I already got this mutha fucka in the full nelson now with this nigga is out they might as well add the figure four leg lock and call me The Nature Boy cause the game just got even dirtier for these other niggas to eat.

"Yeah I know."

"Fam when you going to put me down?"

"You know Unk ain't having it! What you trying to do get me killed."

"I ain't talking about that I'm talking about that flag hanging out yo back pocket."

I don't know what the fuck it is about my flag the attention been on it since I've been home, he's the fifth nigga who has ask to be put on the set. Hell I can't do that but I'll have to ask next time I go out west. The whole damn hood wears red all day, every day, always. I'll see what's up?

"Nah family, you got to earn this!"

"I'm down for whatevea!"

That's the same shit Ty said. They keep playing and I'm a really see if they ready to put in that work.

"Nigga is you ready to kill for this? Is you ready to die for this!?"

He doesn't say shit so I put the press down on him.

"Nigga all these mark ass niggas on TV faking like they down! Them hoe-ass niggas ain't never put in no work! They ain't lost no homies cause of what color he had on! Nigga Crips out number us 10 to 1 that's alot of mutha fucking crabs nigga! It takes heart to be one of us this ain't no mutha fucking fashion show Blood can you digg it!?"

"I can digg it fam sorry."

"Alright then but check it I know you got heart so just set back and wait your turn."

As we were sitting in the back of the house with the big door wide open the next thing I hear was music to my ears.

"Blood you in there?"

"You mutha fucking right I'm in here!"

I jump up and go meet my nigga at the front door.

"Damn it's been a long time since we've been here together."

"You think they ready?"

"Fuck'em if they ain't!"

"Come on I got something for you."

We walk in Unk's room and I fold the mattress back and there was two .380 and Mac-11 and that brand new 9mm.

"All this is for you my nigga."

"Nah blood, this Nina a do for now. But you know I need a chopper."

"That's the one I got yesterday when my people landed. I'll make sure you get that ASAP."

We just stood there for a second but I knew what was coming next so I waited on him.

"Dawg I'm broke and you know niggas talk so put me down."

"I was just waiting on you to say something. But my nigga we ain't dealing with the state no more the shit I got is straight FED time an alot of it if shit goes bad!"

"Time is time blood so it's whatevea."

I went on the closet and got out what I had put to the side for him—a brick of soft and a half of brick of hard.

"Look you owe me 14.5 for this brick so I can pay the plug, but the hard is free it's extras I cooked up from the last batch, of work."

"Damn nigga you got it going on like that?"

He dropped his head and I could tell he was about to say some heart to heart shit.

"Dawg sorry about that night before your parole hearing."

"Yeah that shit's old let it go and listening close. I get 5 bricks every month I could get more we'll have to see but like clockwork there here on consignment I could pay for them up front but why my people never run out."

"I'm in blood all the way."

"I didn't think you go any other way but with me."

"All the way to hell and back my nigga!"

Hell would be a nice vacation to what we were about to embark upon. There would be no turning back now all the chips are on the table and I just pushed me and my main man ALL IN!!!!

CHAPTER - 9

August 29, 2005
Hurricane Katrina makes land fall and
The Bat Phone is ringing once again!

Today's Nicole birthday and I sent her to get her nails and toes done. I been up all morning watching CNN and Hurricane Katrina is ripping the N.O.(New Orleans) apart! Damn I hope my people got up out of there for shit got bad. Bugz had been calling all morning talking about that shit like he is crazy. I look at my watch it reads 1:30p.m. so I picked up my phone to call Nicole to see what time she'll be done cause I'm hungry. Soon as I start to dial but the bat phone rang and I just lost my appetite.

"Yeah!"

"What's popping Damu!?"

"Sometimes you, sometimes me."

"I can digg it baby boy."

"Banks quit beating around the bush!"

"All business, huh? Well I need you here ASAP!"

"Today is baby's birthday can I come tomorrow."

"Nah Blood yo plane leaves at 5:00p.m. from the Greater Cincinnati Northern Kentucky airport."

"Damn Banks, she's going to be hot!"

"Nigga I know she don't run it, so give her some money, kiss her on the cheek and get your country-ass out here "

"I'm on my way."

"Oh yeah bring your homeboy Bugz cause you're going to need a second man to handle this."

"Why can't One be the second man?"

"A real delicate situation, that's why."

"I feel you we're on our way."

"Dawg believe me its well worth your time."

Damn I'm glad this nigga was already in Lexington. Got to call and tell him to go by City Slickers and get something fly to wear. I handled that. Now, it's time for Nicole. Damn! I called her phone.

"Hey baby, when you going to be done?"

"It's going to be awhile I'm waiting to get my hair done right now why?"

"Look before you start tripping my phone rang."

She knows which one I'm talking about so I wait to see her reaction an it wasn't as bad as I thought but she made her point very clear.

"I know your business comes first and I expect that, but sooner or later, I got to come first."

"I know baby, I got you just hold on."

"Now when you leaving?"

"ASAP so I'm a leave a stack on the coffee table and I want you to go out and enjoy yourself. I'll be back as soon as possible okay."

"Come by the shop and kiss me boy before you leave!"

"I'll be through there baby."

I called Scoobie and told him the business on what was up. So he's on his way to take us to the airport. Bugz got here a few minutes ago and I could hear my baby Charlene now.

"Boy you casket sharp!"

That put a smile on my face for a brief moment. Scoobie finally makes it to the spot.

"Bruh swing by Shamiko shop real quick."

We pulled up and I hopped out not thinking as I walked up in a hair shop full of black women. I got all kinds of remarks and complements.

"Damn you look good!"

"She better watch his ass before I steal'em!"

I make it to Nicole and the look on her face is one I'll always remember. She leans over and whispers in my ear.

"You sure you're going to Cali?"

"Yeah baby I'm Cali bound on the next thing smoking."

"Your ass better be!"

"Hold up I got something to show you."

I walked back to the door and waved my nigga Bugz in the shop. Soon as he walks in everybody's mouth hits the floor.

"See I told you."

"You taking him with you?"

"Yeah baby, he's got to go, too."

"Henry you look good."

"Thanks!"

"Look baby we got to be making it. Our flight leaves real soon so you be safe. I love you."

I lean down and kiss her and the look in her eyes was total fear. She's far from dumb so she got a good idea about my trips out west but she'll never really know the truth.

"I love you, baby. Please be safe."

"I know, I'll hit you when we land."

On our way out the shop we see them punk ass Detectives Reeves and Palmer. I smile, Bugz mad dogs them two sucka. I bet their wondering why were so fly? Only if they know that two country boy were on their way to the big city to put the murder game into full effect. Bugz didn't even know it yet but they ass just got put on the list of people to get rid of.

L.A. is beautiful in the day time
but the grim reaper just flew in from Kentucky!

Pusha and Ms. Lady was impressed by our attire but I had to ask them one thing?

"Why ya'll always home when I come out here and not in Pine-Bluff?"

Ms. Lady with her sexy ass answered my question.

"Because country boy your Tone's favorite! I don't know why but you are. Banks asked him the same thing about you an all he would say was you got heart."

Damn Tone got that much faith in me! I can't let him down in no shape, form or fashion.

"I guess I'll have to show everybody else what he sees." Pusha was next on the mic and this shit is real serious from what he was about to put on the table.

"Look Blood the shit that is about to take place is so big that Banks bought home the whole family home. Yeah we here from Arkansas, Darkey'em home from Oklahoma, Peaches 'em is home from Colorado and I can't believe this! I ain't seen these two fools in years myself but Outlaw and Kid is home from Alaska. So get your mind right shit is definitely on my nigga!"

"Ain't nothing we can't handle or Banks wouldn't sent for us. Plus you forgot to mention that Dawg and Bugz are home from Kentucky!"

That put a smile on his face so we kicked it on our way to the spot and can you believe it my nigga Bugz never said one word to nobody. We pulled up at the same house but there were twice as many big boy cars in the driveway as before. Pusha and Ms. Lady lead the way T-Banks was sitting in the chair looking out the window at nothing.

"Dawg this situation is critical!"

"We can handle it Banks or I like told Pusha you wouldn't have sent for us."

"Okay your right well here the business! Do you remember that nigga you got into a fight with when you were at Terre Haute?"

"Yeah I remember that mark!"

"Well Damu he's out and he came home so he got to go!"

"Put me on this nigga's whereabouts and he's a dead man."

"That's the problem! He's running around with the United States Congressmen's nephew and they getting high. The big man said his nephew is becoming a liability so he got to go as well."

"Say no more we on they ass like a cheap suit."

"It's not that easy lil homie they holed up in Mulholland Estates using a armed security service."

"I know you got a plan or we wouldn't even be talking about this."

"Yeah I got one! We got some inside help but we want proof that their dead understand?"

"I can digg it."

"Dawg there's a lot of money and work up in that spot you can have whatever you find but we need them dead ASAP!"

"When we do we get dropped in the hot zone?"

"Tonight Blood!"

"Okay but I need Ms. Lady to take me to the beauty supply shop."

"Nigga this ain't no time to be getting no mutha fucking perm!"

"Nah I ain't! I just need a little something to take with me tonight."

We talked for about an hour. Me and Bugz got dressed in all black. They asked me did he talk. I said no but just then he made a wild-ass request.

"I need a hacksaw."

Killa-T spoke straight up.

"What the fuck you going to do with a fucking hacksaw!? And you Dawg what in the hell do you need a curling iron for!? You Kentucky niggas are crazy-ass a mutha fuckas!"

The drop off was at 11:00p.m. so we had an hour. With two 9mm apiece with Wilson suppressers on them to muff the sound, duct tape, a hacksaw and my curling iron in our position On-One Byrd Dogg and Ms. Lady took us to our destination.,.

Some Nightmare on
Elm St. type shit

My last instructions were to kill everybody in the house.

Even the three crooked security guards. On-One was the only person Bugz talked to beside myself. As we're sitting outside waiting on our green light to go in I look at my nigga and death is all around him.

"My nigga I want to say thanks for being all in with me."

"Dawg you know it's do or die since we were kids, so me coming with you, is like your shadow following you."

"Yeah I know but thanks anyways."

Next thing I knew my phone rang that Banks had give me.

"Yeah!"

"Dawg you're clear. Go up to the side entrance."

"Thanks Blood."

"Dawg, we're counting on you."

"Like I said before that count is good!"

I hung up now without a doubt I knew shit was on. Me and Bugz made are move right before we get there I whispered to him.

"We ain't leaving nobody alive in here tonight."

"That was my plan from the jump!"

This punk-ass security guard let us in. Damn this house was laid out to the fullest. See this neighborhood is for the rich I mean the super rich— movie stars, athletes, congressmen, anybody who had 10 figures or better. Just so happens that's how we got in the gated community in the first place. This is where T. Banks lives inside you could hear music playing loud this is going to be easy. The guard told us they were high as a mink coat and had a couple of bitches up in there with them. It's too bad that some money making bitches got to take a fall they pick the wrong niggas to entertain tonight. Soon as we hit the corner we started blasting. First the guards all three they ass should've been so greedy and maybe they would still be alive. There was four female in here and them two fools were so high they didn't even move.

"Bitch, stop all that mutha fucking screaming!"

She didn't shut up like I said so Bugz pumped one in her head to help her settle down.

"Now does anybody else have a problem?"

By now those two big jerks were well aware of what was taking place and bitch ass Money was the first to speak up. "What the fuck ya'll want!?"

I guess this stupid-ass nigga thinks it's a game! Well we about to show them they just lost everything. Time to refresh his member but first everybody in this bitch is getting duct taped up. Bugz handled that with the help of one of the girls. She was laid back acted like she's done this before too bad she got to die. Once that was complete Bugz shot her in the head. I can't believe this mutha fucka! He lying people to rest up in here well I got something to top all that in just a few minutes.

"Banks said we can have everything we find."

"Dawg we'll be looking all mutha fucking night up in this bitch!"

"I knew you say that here plug this mutha fucka up!"

Bugz just looked at my curling iron with the weirdest look on his black-ass face. Guess he think I'm about to curl one of these bitches hair or something but this one here is for the record books. So I did the shit myself and lean down and took the tape off Money's mouth.

"Fuck you bitch ass niggas!"

"Nah fuck you crab!"

"Nigga let me up so we can catch a fade!"

"What you forgot I busted that ass at Terre Haute!?"

It didn't take long for it to register.

"Man fuck you slob ass nigga I'm going out like a gangsta!"

"Nigga it's too late for that! Oh you must forgot you got Boss and Riverside life you fag bitch!"

The look on his face is one I'll never forget. One of a man who's pride was long gone so I put the tape back over his mouth and I turned my attention to Surfer Boy.

"You going to tell me where's the money and work?"

"There's nothing here so please leave us alone!"

"Too late! You made your choice to run with this sucka so suck it up and ride the wave."

I had to smile at my own stupid little joke but when I looked at Bugz this nigga was all business.

"I swear there's nothing here!"

"I knew you were going to say that but I bet you'll be saying something a little different in a few minutes."

So I covered his mouth back up with the tape. I hope what that old nigga from Nashville said was true.

"Blood pull his pants down!"

"Nigga have you lost your mutha fucking mind!?"

No time to play so I do the shit myself. Pants down and everybody attention on me it was now or never. So I pushed the hot-ass curling iron straight up his ass! Nobody was looking my way now you should've seen the way Surfer boy was straining against that duct tape with veins and shit popping all out his neck. When I looked at Bugz that stupid ass nigga had a smile on his face. Just a few seconds ago he was all business. It's funny how violence can make people smile. I wait a whole minute then I take it out. Now time to re-ask my question, but I didn't need to.

"9-29-3 the wall safe in my bedroom! Before you stick your hand in there type in 3582 so not to set off the silent alarm!"

"See now that wasn't so hard was it?"

"Ooooh. God please don't do that again please! Plus there are 19 bricks in the freezer!"

"My nigga go check, if it ain't where you say it is it's going back in until I cook your inside."

Before he could answer I covered his mouth back up. Bugz was gone for about 10 minutes so I did Money the same way just cause I could. By the time he came back Money punk ass had passed out.

"Dawg you a cold blooded mutha fucka!"

"Yeah whatevea, what you got in that bag!?"

"You remember when we got that $200,000 some thousand out the bank?"

"Yeah, why?"

"I bet this here is way more than that!"

"Yeah well let's clean up time to bail."

"One more thing, Dawg."

"What now?"

"You really think they're going to let us keep all this?"

"Yeah, Banks don't need these little crumbs. Now, are you done with all the questions?"

To answer me, he started shooting the rest of the living witnesses in the head but what he did next took the cake. With that damn hacksaw he been packing around all night in his hands he cut off Money and Surfer Boy heads and stuck them in my Cincinnati Bengals duffle bag.

"God damn it! You owe me a new bag!"

"Awww hell, Dawg. I don't know why you like them bum mutha fucka anyways!? Plus they said they wanted proof they were dead well here's their fucking proof!"

"Let's go and your getting my bag soon as we get home and I fucking mean it!"

"Hold on."

"What the fuck is it now!?"

I watched as this fool shoots the big fish tank that's mounted in the wall.

"Now what in the hell was that for!?"

"You said to kill everything!"

"Boy you are retarded!"

September 1, 2005
On our way home and
going to see someone very unique in my life

On the flight home I sat back looking out my window. Bugz was a sleep and I was thinking about what went down the night we got back to T. Banks house.

"Dawg you take care of that business?"

Without a moment's hesitation Bugz reaches inside my favorite bag and pulled out them two fools heads. Now you would think that all these stone cold killers in this house would have a stomach for what my nigga had just done but I was wrong.

"Dawg what the fuck is wrong with you country niggas!?"

"Banks, you said you wanted proof that they were dead well here's your proof!"

"Nigga I meant a finger or maybe the nigga chain or something else not their fucking heads!"

Ms. Lady ran out the room, Byrd Dogg threw up in the trash can and On-One was just smiling as he helped Bugz hold up them fools heads. Looking at these two all I could do was shake my head cause I knew right then these two were America nightmare young, black and just don't give a fuck about nothing!

"Fuck it! It's way too late for that shit now!"

"Tone picked a mutha fucking lunatic!"

"Look Banks we took care of the problem so chill the fuck with all the crying shit!"

"Your right, blood. You did. But get rid of those fucking heads!" Bugz and One put the heads back in my bag and that shit gets me mad every time I think about those stupid heads in my fucking bag! On-One was standing there with a stupid-ass look on his face, I give him a little hell.

137

"What you looking all stupid for, One. Huh!?"

"I ain't looking stupid, Dawg so stop that bullshit!"

"Well, what the fuck's on your mind!?"

"Nothing, but I'll help him bump heads."

"Good!"

By this time, Byrd Dogg was cleaning himself up but looked my way and said, "Dawg you and your partna 'are some sick ass niggas! You fucking country niggas are out ya'll fucking minds!"

One and Bugz walked out the door. Ain't no telling where the fuck them two niggas are going I just hope they hurry up and dump those fucking heads.

"Are you fucking serious! Did you see that nigga One's eye when those fucking heads came out the bag!? He's just like Bugz. Hell, I didn't cut them heads off, he did. But nevertheless, that's my nigga and I'll die and go to hell about him, so stall us out with that bullshit!"

Banks was looking my way and I knew he was about to start bitching but I was wrong.

"Dawg, listen and listen good! You have a stone killer right there next to you. He'll kill anything you point your finger at. All I ask is you to pull the reins on him from time to time, that's all."

"He's straight, Banks. Real laid back when we're at home."

"I know that's what's so scary about him that nothing seem to matter to him."

Now as I look at my nigga asleep on the plane all I see is my child hood friend. But I knew deep down inside that we both were animals. The copy of the L.A. Times read like this.

"A scene more gruesome than the Manson murders, a South-Central L.A. gang member and the nephew of a United States Congressman found dead. Both of them were decapitated. Four young women were also shot and killed along with three security guards. The heads of the two men were later found on Manhattan Beach."

Yeah they didn't tell you that Money still had that hot ass curling iron still stuck up his ass! Cooked that punk-ass niggas insides. I got a copy for keep sake next stop home.

Later that night

I went to Bugz house cause I wanted to go somewhere other than home. I didn't want Nicole to know I was back plus I had to make Kay keep her mouth shut that we were home.

"Look don't go out lay low for a few days."

"Dawg, where the hell you going!?"

"I got some shit to take care of okay."

I'm going to see Dee. Nobody knows about her she has always been a part of my life. Not even Bugz knows that this is my secret hideout.

I got to tell you a little about her. I went to school with her older sister and when we were young, I use to sneak in her window and stay all night. She got a real good job and any time I call, it's always the same answer.

Now to get my niggas ride, "Give me the key to the Lexus and I need a gun."

He stopped asking all those questions and went and got me a .40 Glock but I could see he wanted to be nosey but he kept it to himself. So I lighting the situation so he could sleep.

"I'll call you soon as I get where I'm going."

"You do that my nigga, I'll stay in until you give me the word."

"Keep Kay busy for me, ya dig?"

"I got her, you be safe."

We hugged and shook up and I hit the door bailing hard-ass mutha fucka cause I'm going to see Dee. On the way to the city (Lexington), I call her. After about three rings, the line goes live.

"Hey baby!"

"Damn what do I owe for this call?"

"Nothing but I'm on my way."

"You know the rules right!?"

"How could I forget them when you tell me the same shit every time I tell you I'm coming!"

"Well I'm waiting on you to say them!"

She gets on my damn nerves with her stupid-ass rules but she treats a nigga like King Tut when he comes through.

"Don't bring yo ass up here if you ain't staying at least two days."

"How can I spoil you in one day or just over night?"

"Okay Dee, I'll be there in a few."

"I'll be waiting daddy!"

"I know you are."

I hung up and turn up Lil Boosie and pop me an X pill. Once to Dee's I knew I wouldn't have to lift finger to do nothing. She wants me naked an in the bed at all times. Before I could even knock on the door she was standing there in her red satin robe and I could tell right away that it's going to be a long two days. I kiss her lips and walk straight past her to the hot shower I know she got waiting on me. Once in the bathroom it's like clockwork I never get to undress myself so I throw my arms up and she pulls my Prada v-neck over my head. She steals a kiss and unbuckles my pants. I step out my Prada flats and she drops pants and my boxers and steps back and has herself a look. Watching her lick her lips makes my soldier start to stand attention. I know she can't wait but I got a trick for her hot ass. I point my finger at the door and she pokes her lip out.

"Why daddy?"

"Can I get a little peace before you eat me alive?"

"I want start nothing let me sit in here with you!"

"No Dee cause you'll end up in the shower with me like always!"

So she started picking up my clothes with her juicy lip poked out; that shit is so sexy. I smack her on her ass and she moaned and turned around and kissed me long and hard. Now I was the one who wanted her to stay.

"Come here baby!"

"Nah I'll wait like you said, but I see somebody who misses me!"

She walked out laughing and I looked down and my dick was rock hard. Fuck it I'm a cool off in the shower for a minute with her smart ass! That's my baby so I'm a give her a pass plus I could hear Lil Boosie playing in the background. See there are two things about any broad that fucks with me. One, they're going to listen to Boosie Badass and two, they a stone cold freak! I've been in the shower for a minute now so it's time to get out. Soon as I pull the curtain back Dee was waiting with a towel in her hand. Damn I didn't even hear her come back in here. All I could do was smile and step into the towel she had ready.

"Thought I told you to get out."

"Quit playing with me baby, you know I got to have every second of you when you're in this house!"

With her and the towel wrapped around me I knew it was on and popping! She doesn't waste any time when I get in this house and I swear I ain't mad at her. She loves to lick on my nipple rings and bite my six-pack like she trying to leave a mark.

"Damn daddy, I missed you!"

"Well show daddy how much you've missed him then!"

The same towel she had just put around me was right back open and she was licking my dick like a ice cream cone! My knees get weak ASAP

141

cause she's putting in major work. I grab her hair and shove all of my dick in her mouth and she expect all of me like my own personal porno star! Damn she knows how to keep me coming after all these years!

"Damn baby, do that shit!"

"You like it, daddy!?"

"Hell yeah, baby!"

"Let momma show you how much I've been missing you daddy, please cum in my mouth!"

"Oooh shit baby, here I cum!"

She didn't miss a drop! She was sucking and pulling on my dick like her life depended on it. She didn't stop and that mutha fucka stayed rock hard and she was smiling.

"Look what I got daddy!"

"What you got, baby!?"

"A hard dick that I need in my pussy!"

We don't even make out of the bathroom. I bend her right over, smash her right on the spot. The pussy is hot and tight and I love every second of it.

"Damn baby, this pussy is good!"

"Yes daddy, give me that dick, don't stop please don't stop!"

I'm straight dicking her down and she's like a wild animal. I know how to send her over the edge so I slap her on her ass real hard and she started shaking so I had to help hold her up cause she cumming all over me!

"Yes daddy, yes!"

"Damn baby, I'm about to cum!"

"Give it to me baby. Cum in momma's pussy!"

As I'm still slow-stroking her, she leans up an I kiss her long and hard.

"I love you, daddy!"

"I know, baby."

For two straight days, we had a ball. I know she going to start that crying shit when I say I got to go and just like when she makes me say the rules about coming to see her, I make her say the rules about me leaving.

"I know you a street nigga and nothing comes before your money, not even family."

"That's a good girl."

"When you coming back, baby?"

"When time permits me to."

With that, I kissed her on her forehead as she watched me hop in my niggas Lexus and smash out. It's my birthday so giving her a little time on my special day will hold her over now time to get home to Nicole. Once there I sat in the car for a minute and checked my voice mail and texts nothing from Redd wonder if she forgot about today? Oh well time to go in the house and see my chocolate baby. When I walk in she had the music up sky high. Jagged Edge song "Promise" was playing as I walked to the back and I caught her fresh out the shower oiling up her body. I just stood there and watched.

"You going to stand there all night or come do what's on your mind!?"

I walked straight over to her and she put her tongue all the way down my throat.

"Damn baby, you miss me or something!?"

"Sometimes I wonder if you're going to walk back through that door that's all baby."

"I can digg it baby."

"Plus, Happy Birthday daddy!"

"What you get me for my birthday baby?"

To show me my present she stepped back, ass-naked. I picked her up and threw her on the bed.

"I love you, baby!"

"I love you."

She said she was my present but it was more like I was her present cause she tapped out after a couple of hours on me trying to knock the lining out that mutha fucka! Now I got her in my arms and she's fast asleep. I lay there starring at the ceiling. So I crawl out the bed and go in the living room. I checked my phone to see if Redd had called or texted to tell me Happy Birthday but nothing. I only person on my text was Bugz.

"Happy Birthday, Blood! Oh by the way I got you a new bag."

That's my nigga! I look at the clock and it read 3:49a.m. Another birthday on the streets in the books. I turned on the TV and cut it down low so I wouldn't wake Nicole. Just then my phone started vibrating so I eased it to ear.

"Yeah."

"Happy Birthday, baby!"

Damn. Redd was on my phone!

"You a little late for that ain't you!"

"Well, at least I called baby!"

"Yeah well thanks! Look I've called several times with no answer what's up?

"I'm in St. Louis."

Now that I think about it she was whispering in the phone. "Yo why you whispering?"

"Look Happy Birthday!"

And just like that she was gone. I tried to call back but it went straight to voice mail. She must be with dude well the next time I talk to her shit going to go one or two ways. My way or no way!

CHAPTER 10

March 7, 2006
Laying a True King to rest!!

Shit been booming non-stop! Money is piling up and me and Bugz been to Cali a lot over the last six months. It ain't just to handle business we robbing all up and down the Pacific 5 highway. I mean catching boss playas with their pants down around their ankles. But today I'll be going to pay my respect to a falling soulja. Foratio got caught up in this mean game that we play in. That's Black's little brother and he's locked up on violation down at North Point, Two he's back on violation down at the F.C.I in Manchester. I'll be making this trip with my nigga Snoop.

I'm deep in my own thoughts when Nicole was talking to me.

"Baby, you hear me?"

"Nah love what you say?"

"It's a little cool out so make sure you put your over coat on."

"Okay baby, go make sure ain't no lint on it."

"Alright, baby."

I slip on my shoulder rig while she was in the back but hell my pistol back there with her.

"Baby!"

She doesn't even answer me she just walked back in with my coat and gun. See this is why I love her so much. I finished getting dressed and I hear a horn outside so I look and it was Snoop. "Later, baby!"

"Boy, you better kiss me before you walk out that door!"

I lean in and kissed her but that sent a fire through my body that I can't explain and I guess she felt it, too.

"Stop baby, I'll be here when you get home."

"Love you!"

"I love you!"

I hit the steps and my Mauri gators made a real smooth sound cause I had the rub bottom on them like a real playa suppose to. Dressed in all black with a red silk tie I hop in the car.

"What's up, big homie?"

"You got it young'un I really can't call it."

"Man I can't believe this shit!"

"You young nigga's in a helluva game now a days, ya'll playing for keeps!"

This shit never matter to me. Hell I've have put other families through the same thing. Now I see from their point of view how shit is all so serious.

"Snoop it seems like yesterday them niggas put me on. Can you believe some Paris niggas putting a nigga on from Georgetown!?"

"New day and time, Dawg shit's changing every day. Them some real niggas over there can't take that from them.

We make the 16-mile trip east on U.S. 460. Once to the church the parking lot was jammed pack. Every D-Boy in central and northern Kentucky was here to pay their respect. Lexington, Frankfort, Richmond, Winchester, Mount Sterling, Nicholville, Cynthiana, Flemingburg, Maysville, and a few other cities were represented here today. Everybody had on some form of red whether it was a t-shirt with Ratio's picture on it or shoes, jackets, ties the service really put some thoughts in my head and every other nigga in this church but we would let all that shit go and get right back to the money. I hollered at Binky and Shawn T and a few other afterward then me and Snoop went to the liquor store and I got two fifths of Grey Goose, one for me and one for Ratio. I was slamming mines back trying to kill it before we got back home and Snoop was shaking his head. I guess he had seen enough so he said something.

"Slow down my nigga that ain't going to bring him back."

"I know but shit's fucked up!"

"Just stay focus on what you're doing understand!"

I didn't say shit the rest of the way home. We made it to our hood and the day had turned out to be nice. I jumped straight out an open the second fifth and give my nigga Black's little brother one more drink on a Georgetown nigga.

"Rest in peace soulja Lord knows a lot of people are going to miss something terrible."

June 10, 2006
Got to clean up my mess ASAP

Finally, all the work and money landed from Cali from all the work we've been putting in out there. We give One a hundred thousand of that money for helping Bugz get rid of those fucking heads! The nineteen bricks plus the five I get every month. OH BOY!

I was sitting around the house doing nothing and my phone rang. I looked at the caller ID and I smile. This number has been the same since I was in high school.

"Hello!"

"Telly, you get your ass down to the house right now!"

"Yes sir I'm on my way."

Damn! I wonder what the fuck got Big Ant in such an uproar? He didn't sound too happy at all. Hope he didn't find out I've been giving Ant that work. I hop in my ride and make the 20 trip down to Burton Pike.

"Hello son!"

"Hey Big Ant what's going on?"

"Look I didn't call you down here to bullshit so you listen and listen good! That girl you left alive is helping the authorities to build a case against you and those other two boys who are locked up!"

I guess I better tell the truth to him ain't no sense in lying cause he already knows too much.

"Big Ant, we had on ski masks so ain't no way she can give them anything that's helpful!"

"Boy, she said she seen those fucking tattoo's on your damn eye lids! Now you tell me how many people walking around Georgetown with tattoo's on their fucking lids!? I'll tell you. One God damn it and it's you!"

I didn't say shit so he kept on raging.

"I tell you what you're going to do! You're going to bring that no good rat bitch down here alive and feed her rotten ass to the hog, you understand me, Telly?"

"I'll handle it, Big Ant."

"You damn well better cause I can't stand to see you back in that fucking cage behind this bitch!"

"I got a plan, I'll be back tonight!"

"I swear to God Telly, you better and I mean it!"

Later that night

I called Ant as soon as I pulled out the driveway of his parent's house. I knew he knew how to find this bitch so I give him an ounce of hard and told him the plan.

"Look bro, shit real tight right now for me this bitch is trying to get me the death penalty."

"We can't have that now can we?"

"No, we can't! So make sure to bring her alive and don't do nothing stupid you hear!?"

"No problem bro! Looks like old times me bailing your black-ass out of a jam."

"This time mean the most Ant!"

"I got you brother, you just be at dad's waiting."

I watched him pull off. Damn, I put my life in the hands of a junkie. I knew one thing for sure, if he didn't br ng that bitch I was turning Bugz loose on his ass! I called Bugz and give him the run down on the play I just called and he was ready. After I picked him up we went down to Big Ant's farm. Once there I told him to wait in the truck I had to go in the house and once I did Big Ant started bitching immediately.

"What in the hell did you bring him for!?"

I didn't say shit I just handed him that copy of the L.A. Times that I bought home.

"What the fuck is this, Telly!? I ain't got no time to be reading no damn newspaper!"

"Just read the front page, Big Ant!"

He grabbed the paper out my hand and I was looking death dead in its eyes.

"Hand me my damn glasses!"

After about two minutes and him shaking his head the whole time he takes his glasses back off and sat back in the chair he was sitting in. The look on his face is one I can't figure out.

"Telly, that was ya'll way out there doing that?"

"Yes sir and I'm in too deep Big Ant and I don't trust nobody but him, you and Ant."

"Son, that made world news. But if ya'll cleaned up so good out there why in the fuck did ya'll leave this bitch alive? Telly, I might as well kill you myself instead of those KKK mother fucker down Eddyville! Hell they love killing you boys down there. Fuck the needle or the chair they wish they could hang your black ass! I love you son. You better tighten up around here, understand me!?"

"Yes sir, I will."

"Good, now do you think you and that boy could handle a few problems for me?"

"Whoever you need out the way."

"I got a few that got to go and I'll pay ya'll very well."

"Nah, they all on the house for you."

"Thanks son, that means a lot to me."

"It ain't that big a deal, Big Ant."

"Go tell that boy I said come on in. Hell, I don't know him but I like him already."

4:30a.m.
Still Waiting!!!!

Can you believe this shit! Ant still ain't made it here yet. Bugz is pacing the floor like a caged animal and Big Ant been trying to call his phone for the millionth time without any luck.

"Telly, I swear I'm going to kill that boy myself!"

"He's coming Big Ant."

"He better for his own sake! Hell I'll take him out his fucking misery smoking them fucking crack rocks!"

I didn't say shit hell I've been giving it to him since I've been home. Just as he was about to say something else Ant's lights hit the driveway. We watch as he took her to the guess house.

"Telly, get that duct tape out the supply closet and some razor blades."

I got what he said and we waited. After about twenty minutes we all headed for the guess house with Bugz leading the way. I knew he would have her in the den that's our favorite place to have fun.

We all hit the corner together and were all business, no games. I hit the lights and that bitch had Ant's dick in her mouth.

"Bitch, that's the last dick you'll ever suck on!"

She thought she seen a ghost. Ant started bitching and complaining like a little girl.

"Man what took ya'll so long!? I didn't want to stick my dick in this bitch's mouth!"

"Aww hell, shut up! Took you long enough as it is!"

She started to try to talk her way out this real sticky situation but I already knew she was as good as dead. Big Ant said it oh so clear that she had to go and I'm not about to go against what he said for nobody.

"Dawg, I swear I didn't say shit to the police!"

Big Ant spoke for the first and his face was fire engine red. "You little lying crack-head bitch! You told them son of bitches every god damn thing!"

"You don't know what you're talking about old man!"

Ant beat me to that bitch! He slapped her in the mouth and I kicked the shit out of her.

"Bitch, don't nobody talk to Big Ant like that!"

"Bitch, you picked the wrong old man to talk to like that!"

She was balled up in a knot on the floor now it was time to clean up my mess.

"Bugz tape that bitch up!"

"Bout mutha fucking time ya'll keep playing with that bitch!"

Bugz and Ant made her strip then duct taped her all the way up. Then they threw her ass in the back of Ant's truck and went to the barn.

The same old scene was playing out right before me. The hogs were crowding the gate cause they knew it was feeding time. Big Ant never had came to the barn when me and Ant be up here handling our business but he was right along for the ride on this one.

"Here boys, throw her ass in the trough!"

After that, with a big smile on his face, Big Ant told Bugz. "Here son take this razor blade and cut her all over her body so them hogs can smell that blood."

We all watched as Bugz did as he was told. Seem like my nigga was really enjoying himself as he cut her up. After about four or five cuts to her body, those fucking hogs went crazy! They were crowding the gate fighting each other for position. Ant hit the feeder button and filled the trough half way just like before. Big Ant had a few choice words for her.

"Bitch, this is what we do to cheese-eating rats! Telly, pop that goddamn gate!"

I barely had the gate open and them hogs rushed out like the Indy 500 had started. She didn't have a chance they ate her while she was still alive. I could see the pain on her face as they were tearing her skin apart and crushing her bones. But you know what? That brought a smile to my face and everybody else was doing the same thing.

They finished her quick and Ant hit the feeder button again so they could finish their morning meal.

I put her clothes in a steel can and sit them on fire. We all went back to the house and had a seat.

"Thanks, Ant."

"No problem bro, I told you years ago we could always get rid of any problems that come your way."

"Yes you did bro and I'm forever grateful for that."

"Look, Telly and Henry keep this to yourselves. We don't need nobody down here in are business understand."

"Yes sir, we will."

"Okay son and before you go take this you know the barn is open to you any time you need it just like before."

"We'll handle this ASAP old man!"

"I know you will son now if ya'll excuse me I'm going to lay down I'm not as young as I used to be."

He hugged Bugz and Ant but hugged me last and whispered.

"Telly kill'em all on that list and I swear by God I want Reeves gone first understand!"

He didn't wait for an answer he just walked off. Little did he know I planning to getting that mutha fucka myself. He just threw gasoline on the fire. We talked to Ant before we left he said he was going to go get some help. I told him let me know anything I can do to help. Me and Bugz were on our way home and I told Bugz the next play and he smiled at the call. "We're going to kill Reeves."

"About mutha fucking time!"

Oct 21, 2006
Going to Cali and not a moment too soon

The call came and believe me it was right on time. Me and Bugz has been putting in work people coming up missing an everybody has their own version of what's going on and our names keep coming up in everybody conversation. We don't give a fuck one way or the other cause if they keep talking they'll be next. Ms. Lady picked us up from Hawthorne airport up near Inglewood and she went to straight running her mouth like only a woman could.

"I hope you two crazy mutha fuckas and On-One don't do that wild shit ya'll did up in Oakland last time ya'll where here!"

I looked at her like she had lost her ever loving mutha fucking mind!

155

"What the fuck is you talking about Oakland for!?"

"Because you niggas are crazy putting that new born baby in the damn oven!"

I thought back to that day and shit was off the chain. Me, Bugz an On-One were dressed up like some Crips and we caught this nigga with his girl and the baby. We were already on him though are people from up that way so once we caught his ass he tried to play hard.

"Nigga where it at fool!"

"I told ya'll niggas I ain't got shit!"

On-One said the damndest thing and caught us off guard.

"Yo cuz go turn the oven on!"

Neither me nor Bugz made a move. This nigga just called us cuz and I damn near blew his head off because I forgot how we were playing this move. We did this so the blood homies in The Bay wouldn't catch on heat behind this one. I guess he seen we weren't moving fast enough to his liking so he went and done the shit himself.

"Bring they ass in the kitchen!"

We made them walk to the kitchen an once there we duct taped them to the chairs.

"Now, one last time, where's the mutha fucking money and the work!?"

"Fuck you crab-ass niggas!"

That shit he said didn't hurt my feeling one bit. One taped their mouth shut and went and got the baby.

"Since you so hard nigga let me see where your heart at!"

I watched as One open the oven and stuck the baby inside. Old girl fell over in her chair fighting like mother should about her children. Dude just sitting there like shit didn't bother him so I grabbed her and pulled the tape back.

"Oh please take my baby out I'll tell you whatever you want, please!"

I open the oven and grabbed the baby and man believe me shit was really heating up in that bitch!

"Now, where's it at, baby girl!?"

"Inside the couch and under the floor board in my closet!"

I watched all the color drain out of dudes face. He didn't give a fuck about his family so right then and there I knew I was going to kill just for fun.

"Go check my nigga an .I swear if it ain't where you said it is lil man going back in for good!"

"It's there I swear!"

She started screaming on old dude so I let her handle her business cause I'm about to kill this clown anyway.

"You punk-bitch! You going to let these niggas kill yo own baby over some money and dope you can get again? You ain't shit I hope these mutha fuckas kill yo ass!"

With that I did her a favor. I pumped two in his head right on the spot she smiled at me. I cut one of her hands loose so she could hold the baby. My nigga Bugz and One came back with a garbage bag full of shit. Damn we came up off that one now back to Ms. Lady.

"Are you serious!?"

"Yeah you need to calm the fuck down!"

I ain't never called her out her name cause I know she'll kill something in a binky of an eye but I lost it.

"Bitch you got some nerve! I didn't say shit when you killed them niggas in Tulsa or Memphis. Let's not forget them niggas in Atlanta who's dicks you cut off and stuffed in their mouths! Oh one better then that, what about that fool in Houston you killed and stuck that big ass dildo up his ass!"

By now she had stop the car in the middle of Crenshaw I didn't know what was coming next but what did caught me by total surprise. She stuck her tongue in my mouth without a care in the world.

"Mmmmm baby!"

She was in another world so I had to bring her back.

"Hey we in the middle of the mutha fucking street!"

"I know!"

She pulled off smiling and shit. Is it me or is everybody that's around me crazy-ass a mutha fucka! But don't get it twisted she's one bad mutha fucka! That's how them niggas came up on the losing end by how beautiful she is. Women be a lot of real niggas down fall.

"Dawg you know my real name so use it okay."

"I hear you baby but what's on your mind?"

"I got to have you in my life that's all."

"What's Banks going to say?"

"You don't know do you?"

"Know what Tonika?"

That's her real name by the way.

"Banks and Tone, 'em are my older brothers."

"Get the fuck out of here!"

"For real, Telly! Tone knows how I feel about you and Banks does too."

"Look you know I got a girl back home, hell two of them for real so what you want to do?"

Now that I think about it I got three cause Dee has always been a part of my life.

"Out here it's just me so I'll take you how ever I can get you."

The whole time Bugz never said one word until now.

"Dawg, you one bad mutha fucka!"

And just like that he went right back to looking at the bright light of The city of Los Angeles.

Kash'd Out

CHAPTER - 11

Today I'm a spend it with my family and go put some flowers on my baby Charlene grave today is her birthday. As I'm getting dressed with Nicole talking my head off, my phone rings. I don't look at the caller I.D. screen, I just answered.

"Yeah!"

"Telly we got a problem I need you down here now!"

"I'm on my way."

Damn shit can't be good if Big Ant is calling like this. I tell

Nicole the business and well meet back here later she really didn't like it to much but shit sounded way to serious not to be on point.

Now time to hit Bugz. After one ring he was on the line. "Get dressed my nigga I'm on my way to get you."

"I'm standing at the door, blood!"

I already knew his response now I'm trying to rack my brain on what got Big Ant in such an up roar. Almost to Bugz's spot and my phone rang again.

"I'm on my way Big Ant!"

"I guess, hello daddy!"

Oh shit this Redd on the phone. Since my talk with her about me or nothing it's been all me.

"Oh hey baby what's on your mind?"

"You! I'm I going to get to see you today?"

"Shit's a little tight baby but I'm a make some time for you okay."

"Tru, that's cool. I'll be back from Maysville later so you be safe. I love you."

"Be sweet baby, I'll see you later."

Soon as I hung up Bugz ran and hopped in the truck.

"Damn Dawg shit sounded bad, what needs to be done?"

"Hell, your guess is as good as mine!"

"Fuck it ain't nothing we can't fix!"

I pushed the speed limit all the way down to Burton Pike. I swung in the long driveway and Big Ant came jumping straight out the front door. Barely one foot out the truck and he was raising all out hell.

"The fucking F.B.I. is talking about raiding my fucking farm!"

"Okay what you want done?"

"Boys Anthony is already up at the barn shit is going to be real messy."

"What you talking about Big Ant?"

"Well son I knew this for a long time but it never matter until now. See the hogs can't digest human teeth so we got to go clean those hog pens out from top to bottom!"

"You're kidding me, right!"

"I'm afraid I'm not, son."

Well I guess you know the outcome of this situation. What you know about wading knee deep in hog shit looking for a mutha fuckas teeth all day! It was so bad the smell is one you'll never forget. I looked at Bugz and I swear shit didn't seem to be bothering him one bit almost like his life depended on it and it really did. Me, Bugz and Ant cleaned those pens out from top to bottom. We found every tooth that was there. 318 that's 10 bodies over the years. Somebody was a couple short. Those pens looked brand new by the time we were done.

Big Ant finally made it up to the barns after we did all the work.

He walked around looking like he was a health inspector from the USDA. I guess he liked what he saw cause he let it show with a smile and a few pats on the back.

"Thanks boys now let those son a bitches come on down!"

"This shit was terrible Big Ant!"

"Well from now on when a problem presents its self you'll have to play dentist all the teeth got to be pulled first understand."

"Yes sir."

"Well hell lets go eat boys!"

He got to be out his fucking mind; go eat! We just got through swimming in hog shit for hours. Ain't no way I could eat a thing. "Nah Big Ant we got to be making it home."

"You sure, son?"

"Yeah I'll be seeing you soon."

"And I'll be here waiting on you."

Later that night....

Nicole is with her family so I've been soaking in the tub trying to get this smell off me. I think it's just in my head but nevertheless I got to get right. I got everything I need in the bathroom with me: both phones, my gun and a big-ass cup of that drink. Lil Boosie was bumping and I was going to see Redd for a little while. Finally stepping out the tub the bat line rang.

"You got to be fucking kidding me!"

I just got home from the farm and now this phone call may have me on the first thing smoking to California.

"Not on Thanksgiving, Banks!"

"Hello baby!"

Well I'll be damn! Tonika is on the phone and I really don't think she should've called this phone. But hell her big brother is the boss so I guess she can do what she wants.

"Hey, what you doing calling this phone?"

"I didn't want to get you in any trouble with wifey."

"I can digg it but what's on your mind?"

"Nothing just been thinking of you since you left from out here the last time."

I'm glad I'm here cause the last time I was out there she wouldn't let me out the bed. She acted like nobody has been in that pussy for years. Plus what takes the cake she keeps her pussy shaved bald! I have a mean fetish for that and freshly pedicured and manicured nails and toes—shit is so sexy!!!

"Look baby, this is what I want you to do. Get a flight and a room in Cincinnati for the 23rd and 24th of December and I'm a come up stay with you, but I got to get home on Christmas Eve, okay."

I had to make sure I see Redd and talk to Dee.

"I'll just stay one night and fly home early Christmas eve."

"Okay doll, you be safe and I'll see you then."

"Okay baby, you do the same."

Now back to my mission and that's getting to Redd's house. I rushed and got dressed and jumped out the front door hitting the steps two at a time. Once in the hood I park my truck and had Turtle drop me off to keep people out my business. I walk straight through the front door and she was standing there wrapped up in a towel.

"Hey, daddy!"

I didn't say shit I walked straight over to her and bite her on the neck.

"Ooooh daddy!"

"What it look like under that towel, baby!?"

"Open it and find out!"

I pulled that towel open and this red mutha fucka had her kitty shaved clean! She knows what to do to keep my attention that's for damn sure!

"You like it daddy?"

"Man hell yeah!"

We make our way to her room and R. Kelly's "Honey Love" was playing and she helped me straight out my clothes. Kissing, biting, touching I mean shit is getting real hot real fast. We stayed at each other for two straight hours until my baby tapped out. I'm still the 13 time world champ. (hahahaha) I got dressed and turned to look at her lying in the bed half asleep but never once taking her eyes off of me.

"What you want for Christmas baby?"

"Just you, daddy!"

"Okay and what else?"

"Surprise me it's whatever as long as I got you."

"I'll do my best, baby."

"Your worst is most people's best so I know it's going to be good!"

Everyday this girl is stealing my heart. I bent down and got me a kiss and a tight squeeze around the neck from her.

"Be safe, daddy."

"I will baby, you be sweet."

When I hit the front steps both of those fag-ass homcide/robbey

Detectives were parked right there plus two city cops. It beats the hell out of me how these two suckas knew where to find me. But damn the only good thing about this was I left my pistol up stairs in Redd's room. Thank God for good pussy cause my mind wasn't on nothing but her. Lord knows I can't stand another pistol case having already been convicted of 922.G that would've been big trouble.

"Happy Thanksgiving, fellas!"

"Happy, my ass!"

That's bitch-ass Reeves talking.

"Is there a problem officers?"

"You're under arrest for 1st degree murder."

"Well let's go so I can call my lawyer."

"We got you and your little black monkey this time!"

"I guess we'll have to just wait and see."

> December 23, 2006
> Case dismissed and
> I'm on my way to Cincinnati!

Can you believe this shit they ain't got a damn thing! No body, no murder weapon or motive, all hear say and a lot of it. Today the judge is going to throw the whole case out due to lack of evidence. People are talking real good now since we've been locked up but they can't quite figure it out. We killing and selling dope well the dope part ain't true anymore because I handed that over to Lil Ty and his crew of misfits(Black one of the triplets, Malcolm, Logik and a few other wild young niggas). My lawyer is going to court today by himself to much media attention. I'm just laying around waiting on my name to be called and my lil homie Tommy Pickles is talking my ears off.

"Damn Dawg you one lucky nigga!"

"I guess my nigga but digg what they going to do with you?"

"Awww hell they give me a state year! I already got 6 months in on it all I need is a number and I'll home."

"I'll be waiting if you want to get some real paper."

"Ain't no mutha fucking question!"

Just then my homie J.T. hit the window he's the Lieutenant at the jail he rolls his hands together that means pack your shit.

"Look blood I'm out break this commissary down with Buddy Red, J-Johnny and Big Nate and send some around on the low side to Taurus tell them fools I'm out.

"That's what's up big homie you be easy!"

"Oh yeah one more thing tell all them niggas we getting money on my streets so if they ain't wit it they ain't welcome!"

I hit the door bailing hard as a mutha fucka! I throw up the set and he hit me right back up soon as I come off the high side my nigga Bugz came bailing off the low side.

"What it B like, Damu!?"

"They can't stop this train, it ain't got no mutha fucking brakes on it!"

"You better mutha fucking believe!"

I-75 North to
The Nati!!!!!!!!!!

I went to moms' house as soon as they let me out. She said my parole officer came by and wanted me to come see her. Ain't likely bitch should've came to the jail if she wanted to see me. Moms said what she had to say and I accepted what she had to say cause her word is gold. I called Nicole and she was crying and really started crying when I said I had to go to Cincinnati until tomorrow. Other than them two bitching at me, a little bit shit went as planned. I'm a see Redd as soon as I get home tomorrow and make sure I hit Dee up just so she can hear my voice then I'm a get on home. But right now it's my California baby doll and I can't wait! On the highway smoking and drinking plus popping X pills shit is about to be on. I get downtown Cincinnati and I call Tonika's phone.

"Hey baby where you at?"

"I'm here but I got to run out to Mill-Ville to see my nigga Fat-C."

That's one of my peoples I meet on my travels through the Federal BOP.

"Okay baby I'm at the Marriott."

"Okay. I'll be there shortly."

"Hey, you strapped?"

"You know I am stop playing."

"Just asking that all."

"Okay, but you be naked when I get there!"

"Baby, I got naked as soon as I heard your voice!"

"Dig that!"

A little while later.

After seeing Fat-C and my nigga LaMont I made it to my destination. Valet parked my truck and the bell hop took me to the top floor and I was smiling the whole way. I knocked on the door and she answered smiling back at me but was standing behind the door so I couldn't see her. I walked in and didn't look back because I could hear her heels behind me and I know that I was in for one helluava surprise. When I turned around, not only was she standing there but so was Peaches. Both of them bad mutha fuckas ass-naked accept their high heels and a dog collar.

"Damn!"

Tonika just smiled but Peaches walked straight over to me.

"You one sexy-ass, country nigga! I had to beg Nika to let me come with her to see you."

"Well you're here, so what you going to do?"

"Whatevea you tell me to do!"

Let me put you up on Peaches. She's part of the family and her and her little crew of females be up in Denver and Colorado Springs and they be tearing them niggas ass out the frame.

"Well since you put it that way put this dick in yo mouth."

She was right up on me so she bite my neck then dropped to her knees with a smile on her face. Tonika came over and kissed and whispered in my ear.

"I love you Telly ain't nothing I won't give you."

She slid down my body to help Peaches with what she was doing.

After five minutes of them licking me to death Nika jumps up.

"Let's get on that big ass bed baby!"

"Hell yeah let's do it!"

I strapped ass naked as fast as I could and jumped in the king size bed with what I would come to find out in just a few moments were two stone cold freaks!

"Nika, let me lick that pussy!"

"Only if you let me put that dick back in my mouth."

Well, we ended up with her on my face and my dick in her mouth. But not to be out done Peaches, took the cake. As I was licking on Nika's pussy, she stuck her tongue right in her ass. She went crazy sucking my dick, so I told Peaches, "Keep licking her ass!"

"I got you baby!"

She was driving Tonika crazy and the head was so good that I shot cum straight down her throat.

"Mmmmm baby!"

Peaches got a little mad with us but I got her too.

"Damn Dawg I wanted, you to cum in my mouth!"

"I got you baby what you going back home tonight or what?"

She just smiled but she didn't know I'm on them X pills so they ass is in trouble. I flipped Nika over and throw her legs on my shoulders and went to pounding on that tight ass pussy. Peaches stole a kiss and whispered a reminder in my ear, "Remember, that cum is mines."

I kept pounding on Nika and she loved every second of it. When I reached my breaking point I didn't even tell her I just pulled Peaches hair and pulled my dick out of Nika and stuck it straight in her mouth.

"Here you go, suck it out me then!"

And suck she did four or five good pulls on my dick I was cumming in her mouth. The show didn't stop there we partied until I could see the sun coming up on The Ohio River. The girls finally give up trying to make my dick go soft.

"Dawg what the fuck are you on!?"

That's Peaches talking Tonika already knows I be on those X pills.

"I ain't on shit! I just beat a 1st degree murder charge an at the time pussy didn't seem like it would be in my future so I'll never take for granted the joys that only a woman can bring."

The look on her face was amazement but I was lying and Tonika was about to steal my shine with her hating ass.

"That nigga lying, girl! His ass be on them purple butt naked ladies that Killa-T been sending him."

"I knew it! Girl that niggas dick never went soft and I know my head and pussy game is on one thousand!"

"Girl that's what got me chasing this nigga all over the country."

170

"Now I'm a be with you."

"You a lie! That was his Christmas present and your's too."

All I could do was smile. All the holiday I've spent behind those walls and fences this one for all the real niggas who ain't never coming home again.

 "Ladies, this was the best thank you."

"We glad you enjoyed it baby but I got you a little something extra to go with this."

She handed me a little red box an when I opened it a big boy set of square diamond earring were looking me dead in my face. She didn't waste any time since I forgot to put a pair on before I left she screwed them right on.

"Thanks, doll!"

"Welcome, baby!"

I lay back with two bad mutha fucka under my arms and every nigga in the world would love to be me but God only made one of so there never will be another me. But the one thing that so special about these two is that they would kill a nigga just as fast as they would give him some pussy.

May 5, 2007
Derby weekend like some of the world leaders
I rule with an Iron fist

We having a cooking out at my spot all my people are coming through so I got to get shit together. I was at my grill cooking and Snoop, Bugz and Lil Ty was sitting around getting their drink on and Snoop was talking shit.

"Dawg you a straight communist you know that!"

"What the fuck you talking about now!?"

"Look my nigga you ain't let up off these niggas since you've been home.

Hustle, hustle, hustle is all you've doing since your feet touched the ground."

"Nigga, I came home dead-ass broke, what was I suppose to do!?"

"Nah lil bruh, it just you working these niggas to hard, give them a day off."

Just then Lil Ty jumped in being rude and shit asking questions that his young ass really ain't ready for the answer to and I really didn't want to give them anyways.

"Yo blood why you got all them tattoo's on your face?"

My mind drifted off for a brief moment. Only if this young nigga knew how me and Bugz have been laying down bodies all over the country. "Young nigga I earned these but I tell you what the one under my left eye is for its real personal. And one day, before I die, whether God has a place for me in heaven or the devil got a spot next to him at his dinner table, I'm going to collect on this debt. The two red ones are for the work I put in for the set all the other shit I'm telling a story Damu now back to your ass Snoop! Is you out your mutha fucking mind? These niggas going to get plenty time off either when they dead or in the mutha fucking penitentiary!"

"That's just it my nigga ya'll going to end up in that bitch for life!"

"Fuck it! You know how I feel about it shit don't stop til the casket drops ain't that right Bugz!?"

"You mutha fucking right, blood!"

"I can digg it then but you still a mutha fucking communist now quit bullshitting on that grill and give me some ribs off that bitch!"

After he said that I thought for a quick second. Some of the world's greatest leaders rule with an iron fist. Fidel Castro, Moammar Gadhafi, Edi Amin even the Oakland Raiders owner Al Davis what they say is the law why I can't do the same in my city.

Later that night

172

Pure luck caught him <u>Slipping!</u>

High ass a mink coat me and Bugz where on our way to the hood.

But I got to go to the Shell's up on Main St. first to get some juice and swisher (grape). I was driving Nicole's car so not to draw to much attention as I was getting back in the car not paying attention to what Bugz was fussing about until I closed the door all the way.

"Look at that punk mutha fucka!"

I looked to my left an I be damn old Detective Reeves was walking in the store. The craziest shit just popped in my head.

"Let's get this mutha fucka!"

"Well what the fuck are we waiting on!?"

"Look, we can't kill him right here so here's the plan."

We had two minutes tops do to what we had to do so we went into action. I went back in the store cause I knew once he seen me he wouldn't be able to keep his eyes off me-BINGO. Sure enough on sight I had him where I wanted him so I went right back out the store cause he was hot on my trail. I walked back over to where the car was parked on the dark side of the store near the railroad track shit is working as plan.

"Hey Mr. Shyne, nice night to put your black ass in jail!"

"Awww man, why you want to fuck up my Derby weekend like that?"

"Cause you're a fucking animal and you belong in a cage and that's where I intend to put your ass for good!"

"Well since you put it that way wait until you see the real animal come out of me."

"What the fuck!"

That was as far as he got Bugz had crept up on him and busted him in the head with butt of his pistol. A little harder then I would've like but fuck this bitch!

173

"Go pull his car around here."

I use his own handcuffs on him as Bugz brought the car around back. We throw his ass in the trunk and I hopped on the phone and called Big Ant it took two time to get him to answer but when he did it was on and popping!

"Hello."

"Big Ant I got him in the trunk!"

"Who son?"

He was still halfway asleep but not for long after this. "Reeves!"

"Okay son, look this is what I want you to do!"

"I'm listening."

"Who's with you right now?"

I started the go bananas on Big Ant! Ain't but one nigga I would have with me when I'm about to kill a cop.

"Bugz why!?"

"Leave him there son I got some people who are going to want to see this and you're the only one they want to see understand!"

"What the fuck you mean other people want to see this!?"

"Look son this is bigger then you could ever imagine but I'll explain it to you later now get your ass down here!"

"I'm on my way."

Bugz heard the whole conversation and believe me he was none too happy about it.

"You ain't going without me Dawg!"

"I got to my nigga so take Nicole's car home for me."

"Man hell nah I'm going with you Blood!"

"Look my nigga we ain't got time to argue so do like I asked!"

We're locked eye-to-eye and now I see what the world is scared of—a young black man with no regards of human life not even his own. But here the catch there is a million more just like him.

"If you ain't back by 8:00a.m., I'm coming down there and kill everything!"

"I know you will but trust me Blood!"

As we were standing there talking my peoples who lives down that way came by. Star was blowing and waving so I blew her a kiss and she kept it moving on about her business.

"Look my nigga we been laying mutha fuckas down from here to the west coast but ain't no turning back after this one."

"Fool I've been had tunnel vision! Fuck that cracker in the trunk and anybody else in our way!"

"I'll hit you later."

"Do me one blood?"

I stopped and looked my nigga in the eyes and I seen death all in them damn I'm glad this my nigga and not my opposition.

"Yeah my nigga what is it?"

"Make sure that mutha fucka dies slow."

"You better know it."

"It's a cold world blood!"

I finished his sentence.

"No mercy!"

Down on the farm

I took my time getting there so by the time I did pull up Ant was sitting on the porch waiting.

"What's up bro?"

"Got some business in that trunk."

"I know so let's go on up to the barn."

We go up to the barn it's early and the hogs are up moving around cause they know it's feeding time.

"Pop the trunk bro!"

I opened the trunk he was still knocked out from the blow Bugz put on him. I smiled cause I guess that was a little get back from busting him in the mouth at the county jail when they picked him up about that murder sometime back.

"Throw some water on that bitch!"

"Nah lets hang him on the hooks first."

We got him up on the hooks real mean looking things these hooks hold 800 pound dead hogs so his ass was like a feather on it.

"Dawg, let me warn you about something."

Before he could finish, in walked Big Ant, the county prosecutor and two of the biggest local business men—the dentist and the mutha fucking mayor! I pulled out my pistol and pointed it at the crowd.

"Big Ant I can't believe you set me up like this!?"

"Calm down son, it ain't what you think!"

"Well what the fuck is it then!?"

I knew one thing was for sure I was about to get to busting in here.

"You better talk to me Big Ant!"

"Son all these gentlemen are my business associates. We all have real high stakes in a lot of other things that are well let's say a little shady. That piece of white trash over there was helping the feds build a case against us. I can't spend the rest of my life in one of those hell holes they had you in."

Now as I look back and forth between everybody standing in the barn it all finally came to me. Everybody whose name was on that list is standing right here accept the mayor. Damn Big Ant is to good we about to kill everybody all at once.

"Now put that damn gun down before you shot me cause I'll be mighty pissed at you!"

I lowered my gun but I didn't put it away. Ant slid his goof ball ass right over next to him.

"Sorry bro I tried to tell you."

"Well what the fuck took you so long!?"

He didn't say shit as all these crooked ass hillbillies started shaking my hand and smiling and shit. The punk ass detective started moving around Big Ant told me and Ant.

"Boys please strap that rat mother fucker!"

We cut his clothes off him so by now he knows shit is way past serious.

"I knew all you trailer trash mother fucker were up to no good!"

"Well I guess you were right and see what being right has got you."

"If you let me go now, I'll forget any of this every happen!"

"Too late, you sorry son of a bitch! Telly, you and Anthony remember what I said about all teeth got to be pulled first?"

"Yes, sir!"

"Well the good old dentist here is going to see if either of you have a career at it."

The laugh I heard around the room from all these white men let me know one thing they all were killers. Old Reeves I guess knew it was a wrap so he let all his racist side really show.

"All ya'll some goddamn nigger-lover, sons of bitches! Going to let this little ugly monkey do this to me?"

Big Ant said the damndest thing I've ever heard. I didn't like but I had to smile.

"I tell you one thing boy! That's one crazy nigger but I love him like he's one of my own so that makes you shit out of luck! Now boys do like I told ya'll!"

Ant grabbed a set of pliers and I squeezed his jaws. He put up one helluava fight until Ant snatched that first tooth out his mouth then one by one we took turns. Hell this punk passed out no way I'm a let him miss one second of this I walked over and turned on the water holes

"Nah bitch wake yo ass up!"

I sprayed ice cold water in his face to make him come back for the rest of the show it's going to be real good. After all his teeth were in the pan the dentist came over and had a look for himself.

"You know Big Ant both these boys could work for me."

They all laughed but Big Ant shot right back.

"Hell those boys ain't but good at one thing and that's killing!"

"That ain't hard to believe hell you schooled them on the fine arts of how to do it."

Now that really puzzled me with that statement. Big Ant called us over to the side.

"Look here boys after ya'll get through I want everybody dead accept the mayor understand."

"Yes sir."

We walked back over to where Reeves was hanging and he was crying and mumbling to himself. Ant brought over two bowie knives I remember these things from when we used to go deer hunting back in high school real mutha fucking sharp. I grabbed his leg and locked eyes with the man I was about to skin alive.

"Ant looked at those hogs over there waiting on us to feed them!"

"Well, what the hell are you waiting on!?"

He opened the gate and they rushed the trough their huffing, biting and pushing each other out the way cause that smell of blood had drove them mad.

"Hey Reeves remember when you called me an animal early tonight? Well you were right!"

I cut a big hunk of meat out his leg and throw it to the hogs. He watched as they ate a piece of his leg. Now Ant cuts some of his arm we were butchering him alive. I hit the feeder button and let the trough feel halfway up. We took what was left of him and throw him in so the hogs could eat. I looked at Ant and we spun around and started shooting everybody Big Ant said to shot. Four more bodies we had to strap and pull their teeth. By now Bugz is blowing up my phone so to make it stop I answered it.

"What!?"

"You okay my nigga?"

"Yeah I'll holla when I get home."

And just as fast I was back to doing what I was doing and Big Ant and the mayor just sat back like nothing was going on. We just killed the county prosecutor, a robbery/homicide detective, two of the biggest businessmen in town and the mutha fucking dentist. Ant never said one word the whole time, so the mayor came over to us.

"Thanks boys, I owe you one."

"Don't mention it cause it wasn't for you!"

He didn't say shit just turned and walked back over to Big Ant and they talked for a quick moment then he left. Big Ant came over to where we were finishing up the last of our work.

"Thanks boys ya'll saved my ass I love ya'll!"

"We know."

"Look we'll take all these cars to my brothers salvage yard in Mt. Sterling after we take them up on the back of the farm and burn them up."

One thing was on my mind and I couldn't let it go without saying something.

"Big Ant what about the mayor?"

"Awww hell boy he loved your daddy something terrible. Said he could play the hell out of basketball when he coached him in high school."

"Think he'll tell?"

"Nah son I really don't. He's in just as deep as we are."

"If you say so but I swear to God I'm going to kill him if I even think he's going to turn on us!"

"If anybody knows what you're saying is the truth I do."

"Well as long as you know."

"All too well son, all too well."

CHAPTER 12

July 8, 2007
A weekend of pure fun!

Me and Nicole ain't seeing eye to eye right now on some things so I got me a little spot. Ain't what you think a boss nigga like me should have but can't nobody put me out. She's still my girl but to many people in her ear, but right now I got Redd on my mind. It's early in the morning and I know she's on her way to work. I'm still in the bed from the night before, drunk as hell! My phone beeps and I know I got a text from somebody so I struggle to roll over. But I got to get up anyways cause my sister Simone is on her way to get me, so we can go get a rental. Phone in hand eyes half open and a smile appears instantly.

"Hey daddy I can't wait til tonight I LOVE YOU!"

Looking at the ceiling thinking I can't wait to see her either. I get on up and got dressed by the time I was done Simone was blowing her horn all crazy and shit. We got straight on the highway and she started nagging me like a mother hen.

"Damn boy you smell just like a damn brewery you stink!"

"Had a long night big sis, so cut me some slack."

All night in Mr. Robert Earl's spot gambling and drinking with them old niggas well do it every time she just shook her head. We make it to the rental place and I pick out a Chrysler 300 and rode out bumping Lil Boosie going straight to the mall. I finally make it back to my spot to lay down for a few minutes. A few hours later, I jumped up and got fresh cause I got to get my hustle on.

Today the price is going to be even cheaper then I already got it cause everything I make I'm blowing it this weekend cause tomorrow is Redd's birthday. I was kicking it with Bugz when Lil Ty dropped off ten stacks from what he did last night. Now time for Bugz to be nosey.

"Dawg, where's your bags at my nigga?"

"Don't need none. I'm buying everything brand new when I get there you feel me!"

"Play hard blood but dig, bring me something back."

"I ain't going nowhere but to the Nati."

"So what I still want something!"

"I got you my nigga now let's ride to the L."

"I thought you'd never ask!"

We go to the liquor store, I got a fifth of Grey Goose and some grape swisher. I got an ounce of that purp on the way back I give him the run down but I waited until last when I told him this weekend's ticket for the young niggas cause I knew what he would say. As I dropped him off, I let it fly.

"Be safe my nigga!"

"No doubt but tell Ty'em the ticket is $500 hard and $650 soft but only until I get back."

"See that's their fucking problem now! You spoiling them young niggas to much make them lose that hunger that they need!"

"They'll be alright hell we can't make all the money!"

"We can damn sure try!"

With that I pulled off smiling this weekend is going to be fun. I throw in my Jim Jones CD and make my way to Redd's house I pulled up and made the call.

"I'm outside baby."

"Okay daddy I'm on my way!"

I could hear the excitement in her voice and that made me smile. I popped two X pills real fast before she got in because she always gets on me about trying to stay in the pussy all night. I watched her walk out with some short shorts, flip flops and those big ass titties fighting for position in that tight ass shirt. She got in and the smell was so intoxicating I lost myself in her.

"Hey, daddy!"

"Come here baby!"

She leaned towards me and give me a kiss so soft and sweet that I couldn't wait to get her to the room.

"Here put some fire on this."

I seen the look she give me and I know without a doubt her attention was mines. I put Lil Boosie back in cause she loves that shit and we rode out into the night. We made it to the hotel and I go in and fuck with the old man that's always at the counter for a few minutes. After that, I parked and grabbed her bag and we went in the room. The first thing she does is cut on that damn air conditioner I grab the remote and cut on the TV.

"Damn baby. I got to go to the store. I need some ice and juice; you going or what?"

"Yeah daddy, I'm going. I'm not letting you out my eye sight for the next 48 hours!"

"Bullshit, you just want a Mountain Dew and a Snickers."

The smile I got is the one I love to see. We hopped back in the ride and went across the street to the Pilots. I got a 44oz cup of ice and some orange juice plus some more grape swishers. As she came around the corner I saw what she had in her hands she so predictable but my baby.

"I told you that's all you wanted!"

"And you daddy!"

She kissed me right on the spot and that made my dick start to get hard cause the feeling she gives me is unexplainable an I love every second of it. Back to the room I make me a drink and start putting water in the hot tub because if I let her do it, shit would be so hot you could boil lobster tails in it. I hop out my clothes and she never once took her eyes off me. From the look on her face I knew I was in for one helluva night. After I had eased my way in the water I forgot every damn thing I need.

"Baby, bring me my drink and one of those blunts."

She walked over and gave me my stuff and started undressing. I couldn't keep my eyes off her that honey red skin made my mouth watering. Once she was out of everything those tan lines had me wanting her right now! I hit the blunt real hard a couple of times and watched as she got right in,

"Awww daddy, this water is cold!"

I swear I knew she was going to say that shit!

"Well put some hot water in it then cry baby!"

Shit was already hot as a mutha fucka! She cut the water on and came and got right in my lap. Her in one hand and my drink in the other I can't think of no better place to be right now. "Stand up daddy I want to play with you!"

"Only if you play fair."

The smile that appeared on her face let me know I was in some good trouble. Them damn X pills were working magic so the party was on and popping! I stood up and she wasted no time licking and kissing all over me. Looking down at her made my knees weak.

"Damn baby that shit feels good!"

"Mmmmm daddy, sit back down! I got you all night so I ain't in no rush to do nothing. Plus, finish your drink and what I tell you about popping them damn pills!"

I just smile at her.

"You kill me trying to stay up in this pussy all night you no better!"

I know she was playing hell she can't get enough of me when we're together. We finished the blunt and I knock my drink down and those fucking X pills were working overtime on me.

"Let's go have some fun baby!"

"You going to let me finish what I started?"

"Yeah baby after I have me a taste of that candy!"

I got out first cause Ilove to see her body when it's wet. As soon as she got on the bed I didn't waste a second. I kissed her hard and the low moan that I heard drove me crazy. On my way to the pussy I stopped to suck on those big titties and then I finally make it to my destination.

"Stop daddy I'm already wet down there!"

"So what? That's even better for me!"

I spread her legs wide and the wetness was visible because that pretty pussy was shaved bald, tongue first I go. As I look between her legs she had her eyes closed and squeezing the sheets I kept licking harder and faster.

"Yesss daddy lick that pussy!"

I licked that pussy until she started shaking I didn't waste any time I slide straight up in her and pulled her hair at the same time.

"Ooooh shit daddy I'm cumming again!"

"That's what I like to hear!"

We were at it for hours. I looked at the clock it read 1:57a.m. (7-9) it's her birthday. I was still up in that pussy and she had her legs wrapped around me.

"Happy birthday, baby!"

"Thanks daddy!"

"What you want for your birthday?"

See whatever nigga had her before me didn't teach her right.

See I got her sex game up and she does everything I like. I was slow stroking her and she was making fuck faces and moaning as she was trying to tell me what she wanted.

"What I want is for daddy to cum in this pussy!"

Damn she knows how to get me there now time to stand up. I throw her legs on my shoulders and went to smashing that pussy. Five straight minutes of us talking shit back and forth I was at the edge.

"Who pussy is this!?"

"It's yours daddy now please cum in this pussy please!"

I busted all in her she never let me move one inch. Her legs stayed around me until my dick went limp inside her. I rolled over and she crawled right up on me. "I love you daddy!"

"I know baby I love you!"

A few minutes later her breathing was light and I knew she was fast to sleep. For me sleep wouldn't be easy I got a bad feeling shit is coming to end one way or other.

September 2, 2007
Labor Day weekend and
It's my birthday again!

I just got back in town me and Redd been hanging real tough these last few months. Nicole is still in my life but now I got to make time for her. She works at one of the security gate at the Toyota plant. I blew a lot of money this weekend now time to go check the trap. I drop Redd off at her house and I make my way to the hood. It's nice out and everybody is out kicking it and since my birthday is tomorrow I'm going to set it out. I pulled up Bugz and Scoobie were sitting out getting their drink on.

"What's up bruh?"

"Nothing, just enjoying life that's all."

"I heard that but digg you going to the party tonight?"

"Hell yeah I wouldn't miss it for the world!"

Just then Bugz jumped in.

"What you bring me back!?"

It's my day and this nigga asking what I brought him back. He knows I got something in this truck for his black ass.

"Nigga please! Is that all you know? I didn't bring you shit back this time!"

That nigga walked straight past me and went in the back of the truck and went to going through my bags. I knew it wouldn't take him long to find those size 10 J's monkey ass nigga.

"Thanks, bruh!"

"Yeah my nigga you welcome!"

Just then Mailman pulled up. His truck sounded like he got a marching band it that bitch. He had that Plies on that one song "100 years" I heard a line I would never forget.

"Ain't talked to me dog yet I know he's sick the next 15 years of his life nigga behind the fence!"

The thought of going back to the belly of the beast was a sobering one. Who would hold me down, who would make those long-ass trip to see me, would I make it back home alive this time? Just as fast as those thought hit my mind they exited just as fast. Right now is all I'm living for we'll worry about that shit when it comes my way. I pulled out two liters of Grey Goose and a couple bottles of Moet' and to top it all off I throw about two grand up in the air. Ball til you fall is what I was told and I swear I've been balling hard since I hit the streets. Everybody was having a good time as the sun started going down and people were headed home to get dressed for the party but not me. I was already dope boy fresh Coogi from head to toe and the brand new Sprite can J's on my feet. Me and Bugz were kicking it and my phone rang I look at the I.D. screen it was Nicole.

"Yeah!"

"Hey baby what you doing!?"

She knows I hate when she does that but my heart stills lets her make it.

"What I'm I always doing baby!?"

"Oooh you don't have to be so mean all the time!"

"What you want, baby? I thought you were at work."

"I am but I'm hungry."

"You want me to bring you something to eat?"

"Please!"

"What gate you at?"

"Five, baby. Will you bring me some KFC."

"Okay I'll be there in a few."

I hung up and Bugz was getting ready to say something but I stopped him in his track.

"Don't start okay let me do this!"

"Look my nigga I got to say this! Both of them girls love the fuck out of you don't know why but they do. So go easy with their hearts blood you know how shit goes."

All my life I've never heard this fool ever say no shit like that I guess all the death we been spreading around got my nigga going soft. Nah I really doubt that.

"You done yet with your nosey ass!"

"Yeah I'm done I'll meet you at the party."

I hopped in my truck and smashed out. I got Nicole's food and was on my way to give it to her and my damn phone wouldn't stop ringing. So by the time I got to her that bitch went dead thank God! Shit seem real slow when I pulled up on this beautiful Sunday even so she came out the booth.

"Here baby, I got you a two piece."

"Thanks baby, why don't you sit with me for a minute please." Damn I know she's about to start with that bullshit but she didn't truth be told she damn near caught me off guard with what she said.

"When you coming home?"

"You put me out remember."

"I know baby I was mad at you about all the shit I've been hearing."

"Hearing is your problem! All those lonely no man having bitches you be running with got you mad at a real nigga who give you what you never had."

"And what's that?"

"I loved you for you."

"Yes you did."

"Plus baby you ain't no angel."

She dropped her head see I run these streets ain't no secret safe out here.

"I'm sorry okay!"

"Yeah baby I am too but digg let me ask you something? How you go from fucking with the boss to fucking with the help?"

I knew as long as I was on God's green earth she would never able to answer that question. And believe me that's cool cause I helped play a role in how our situation had became what it has.

"Well baby I got to go you straight?"

"I guess I'm I going to get to see you tonight?"

"Yeah you will only if you come find me."

"Where you going to be?"

"If you really want to see me you'll find what you want."

"Telly do you love me?"

"Like I told you before until they cover me with dirt baby."

I kissed my baby real soft and seen tears form in the corners of her eyes.

"I hope you find me tonight baby!"

"Don't you worry I will!"

I got back in my truck and hit the gas. Lil Boosie was playing and I was in another world I could feel the belly of the beast pulling me back in.

Later that night
My last party before they close
the doors behind me for decades

The party was in full swing when I got there the whole hood was up in this bitch. I could smell the finest weed being blown.

I see my people drinking on the best liquor money could buy. L.H. had the party, jumping and everybody was on the dance floor. I played the back cause my pistol was in my pocket but it looks like I won't be needing it tonight. A cup full of syrup and two X pills in my body I was feeling good. Bugz was standing next to me with Mailman and Pretty Toni talking shit like always. I watched Randi walk by and I winked at her and she winked back that brought a smile to my face and hers too. But as I look I see Dee coming straight towards me with that devilish grin on her face so I sit back and wait to see what's on her mind. She walked straight up on me and without hesitation kissed me right in front of these three fools. I ain't mad. Hell, I'm a playa, that's how it goes. She didn't say shit and turned on her heels and went back the way she had come. I can't lie, it felt real good to be around all my people without no drama, nobody acting a fool just having a good time like we suppose to do. As the night went on the clock hit 12:01a.m.

September 3, 2007 I can't believe I made another one alive and on the streets. About twenty minutes later Shay-Shay came over to where we were kicking it.

"Bruh, Nicole said she's outside."

"Oh yeah! Well go tell her I said to find me herself."

"Okay, bruh!"

I watched her go back the same way she had just come. Not two minutes later, her and Nicole walked up and grabbed my hand. On our way out I stopped to talk to Bugz.

"Look my nigga no matter what happen to me remember it don't stop until the casket drops."

"On my life the flag will never hit the ground!"

"I know it wouldn't my nigga you be safe and take the truck with you."

"I got it my nigga holla if you need me."

Just then Nicole tugged on my hand so we walked out the party I don't know what going to happen after tonight but right now I was in the moment.

Nov. 2, 2007
Kash'd out from the game!!!!

I woke up early this morning and just laid there looking at the woman laying beside me asleep. Redd was knock out so I kissed her on her neck and she moaned real lightly. "Hey baby I'm about to go to Bugz house."

"Not yet, daddy!"

Damn she pulled me straight on top of her so I put in some work after that I was getting dressed as she laid there looking at me. I wonder what's on her mind. I guess I better find out before I walk out this door. "What's on your mind baby?"

"I got to tell you this before I lose the nerve. Telly I'll always love you even when I'm mad at you or you're far away."

I looked at her without understanding of what she was saying. It would take some years but I would come to find out she is a 100% thoroughbred something every real nigga needs when it's time to go back behind these walls and fences. I walked over and kissed her then eased my way out the door without looking back. I went to Bugz's house and bull shitted for awhile then through the hood to check the trap. Redd was gone to work by the time I got back to the spot so I got myself together so I could go handle some business. Damn why didn't I take this 227 grams of hard with me this morning! That young nigga was suppose to come get this shit last night or I would've never brought that shit with me. I made a few calls then I got back in traffic and I swear it seemed like nobody was on the road but me. I turn under the tracks and blow as I pass my grand-momma's house then turn right on Payne St. My little cousin Turtle was waiting on me on the front side of the park. I turned left on Marks Street and I see him park right there waiting in his El-Camino. Once I pulled up, he jumped in the truck with me so I turned to him playing.

"Where's the green at young nigga!"

"I got some hold up!"

He dropped his head for a brief moment and when he looked back up I thought he seen a ghost. All the bad shit I've done ran through head so fast that when I went to reach for my gun it wasn't there.

So I turned to look my killer in his eyes, but there was none. Death might have been better than what these crackers had in store for me. I knew right then and there it was over for me. Every mutha fucking police in the town was around my truck! Damn all the work was inside this Coogi track jacket I had on.

"Put your fucking hands where we can see them or I'll blow your head off!"

I know this hillbillies wanted to do just that but I think I'll get with him on another day Lord willing. Face down on the street with the cuffs super tight they found the work. Acted like they hit the lottery or something hell that ain't even 1% of what they let in the country every day. Once down to the county the news was blurring about my situation and shit wasn't as bad as they put it. Me being who I am I just pressed the bunk because I knew one thing was for sure.

THE GAME WAS OVER FOR ME.

ABOUT THE AUTHOR

I must say it's been an absolute pleasure for "ME" to represent for my "TOWN". I want you to know they know about us in L.A., New York, D.C., Chicago, Miami, New Orleans, Little Rock, Baton Rouge, Pittsburgh, Philly, Denver, Columbia South Carolina, Birmingham, Charlotte, Winston-Salem, Cincinnati, Dayton, Cleveland, Kansas City, Atlanta, Athens, Houston, Seattle, Nap-Town, Memphis, Detroit, Nashville, Richmond Virginia, Dallas, Las Vegas, Charleston West Virginia, Albuquerque New Mexico and all the Common-wealth of Kentucky.

I swear I could go on for days but I'm not but there are more places that know about "US" because of "ME". I want all of you to know that I PUT ON FOR MY CITY. When I say this, I say it with PRIDE because I'm not ashamed of where I'm from because I am GEORGETOWN KENTUCKY until the death of me. You still can't stop my SHYNE!!!!!! !!!!!!!

You may order more copies of this book and/or copies of Tyrene "Topp Dawg" Collin's first book, All In, The Bluegrass Story, Part I, using this order form or logging onto:

MidnightExpressBooks.com

QTY	Title	Price Each	
_____	All In, The Bluegrass Story Pt. 1	$10.95	_____
_____	Kash'd Out, The Bluegrass Story, Pt. 2	$12.95	_____

Shipping

____ books ordered @ $3.99/Each _____

TOTAL ENCLOSED _____

Please send check or money order to:

Midnight Express Books

POBox 69
Berryville, AR 72616

NAME: _____

ADDRESS: _____

CITY: _____ STATE _____ ZIP _____

Shyne Bright Entertainment's
Up and coming titles:

Let's Get Even – the Bluegrass Part III

Chasing the Gingerbread Man

The Preacher and The Dope Lady

Available titles:

All In – the Bluegrass Story